"I'd like t̲o̲ ... r you as y̲o̲ ... ."

Anna's voice t... ...she saw the frigid look on Dusty's face.

"You expect *me* to hire *you*, a pint-size woman who's trained—what? A few working cutters?—to manage my stables?"

The mocking incredulity in his voice made Anna flinch, but she'd come here expecting to be rejected... at first.

"Even a pint-size trainer is better than nothing," she challenged. "You need me, and I can start tomorrow. Where do I put my things?"

Dusty plunged his hands into his pockets, muttering, "Hell."

The hushed blasphemy was stark proof that Anna was going to have to cope with a rotten situation. Honestly wanting to make everything work out, she offered, "I realize hell is where you'd like the entire Andrews family to go, but for now, where do you want me to put my things?"

He raised an eyebrow, considering her. "Miss Andrews, if you're half as smart as that mouth of yours, you just might last out the week."

Howdy to all you Harlequin Romance Readers,

I'm happier than a bear with a new honeycomb to be a part of the Back to the Ranch series! I've been a cowboy fan since the days when I refused to go to ballet class on Saturday mornings because I'd miss the Roy Rogers show.

I'm sure my loyalty to good ol' Roy is the reason I'm *not* a prima ballerina. (Well, I can tell it that way, can't I?) Needless to say, I'm still a Roy Rogers fan. And I'm still a cowboy lover. I'm crazy about those boots and spurs, those brokenhearted country tunes. And a "howdy ma'am" makes my pulse race every time.

Even though I can't ride a horse worth a darn and I always seem to be the first rider scraped off under a low branch, that doesn't mean I don't thoroughly appreciate the way a *real* cowboy (or cowgirl) sets a saddle. And I'll certainly never tire of the way my own slow-drawling cowpoke grins and flirts and two-steps me across the floor in his thigh-huggin' jeans.

I love the lullaby of crickets on quiet, clear nights, and the bright, yellow moon shining down over my "green country," Oklahoma. This is where I was born. A place I'll always love and call home. It's a haven full of honest, good-hearted people, a mixture of old-time cowboy guts and Native American pride—a winning combination.

So, I say, thanks again, for being allowed to show off a bit of my home state and its straight-shootin' folk. Oh, and one more thing—I'll be as happy as a kitten full of cream if you enjoy my story!

My best to you all, or as Roy would so eloquently put it, "Happy trails to you!"

Renee Roszel

DARE TO KISS
A COWBOY
Renee Roszel

Harlequin Books

TORONTO • NEW YORK • LONDON
AMSTERDAM • PARIS • SYDNEY • HAMBURG
STOCKHOLM • ATHENS • TOKYO • MILAN
MADRID • WARSAW • BUDAPEST • AUCKLAND

To
Denise Marcil—
and it's about time!

ISBN 0-373-03317-6

DARE TO KISS A COWBOY

CHAPTER ONE

ANNA HAD NEVER EXPECTED to be standing in the grand foyer of the main house of the famous Bent River Ranch—certainly not for this awful reason. It was deathly quiet, and she shivered, more from anticipation of the scene to come rather than the coolness of the air-conditioning. Her stomach twisted with anxiety as she envisioned how Mr. Dare would take the news that she was waiting to see him.

The very idea that she was here because her brother had stolen from Mr. Dare tore her up inside. To pay off a gambling debt no less! She squeezed her eyes shut, still not wanting to believe it. What could Steven have been thinking? Clearly, he hadn't been thinking at all.

Unfortunately her brother had always been a me-first, hotheaded young man, all too like their father. Steven's rashness had gotten him into lots of trouble when he was growing up. But Anna had thought—hoped—he'd outgrown it.

Before he left home two years ago, Steven had become an excellent cutting-horse trainer, with visions of being a big-money winner, like their uncle Bud had been twenty years before. But the national spotlight hadn't come fast enough for Steven's ego, so about a year ago, he'd decided to get rich quick—by gambling. He'd won some, but he'd lost, too. And his losses had been greater than his wins.

When she and Uncle Bud were forced to put a second mortgage on the family ranch to cover the debt, Steven had promised he wasn't going to gamble anymore. He'd sworn he'd get help. But last night, when Mr. Dare's lawyer had called, looking for Steven, Anna had been horrified to learn that Steven was still gambling, and in deeper trouble than he'd ever been before.

She glanced around, trying to calm herself as she took in the grandeur of the imposing entrance hall. Painted a pristine white, which contrasted nicely with the dark polished stairs, railing and floor, the place spoke subtly of wealth. Two white Corinthian pillars soared to the high ceiling, and just behind them, in an artistic counterpoint, the serpentine curve of a spiral staircase streamed upward past a second- and third-floor landing, to a belvedere at the top of the house. At least, that was what Anna had read once in a national architectural magazine article about the place. All she could see from her vantage point was the spiral staircase leading up beyond the first floor. She hadn't dared intrude far enough into the house for a better look.

Glumly dropping her gaze to her scuffed boots, she prayed she'd see more of the house—and that Mr. Dare wouldn't simply have her thrown off his property without listening to her proposition.

"DUSTY, BOY?" A familiar scratchy voice broke into the master of the mansion's surly thoughts, adding cautiously, "I need to talk with ya, son."

Dusty Dare had swiveled his leather chair away from his desk to face the windows.

"Dusty?" Max said again, sounding troubled.

Wearily Dustin turned in his chair. The old codger standing in the doorway looked about as unhappy as a man could look without a bullet hole in his gut. He appeared even more bowlegged than usual, if that was possible, in his ill-fitting tuxedo. And his weathered features were so miserable the curse that had made its way to Dusty's lips died there. The old hand was loyal, and he loved Dusty like a son. He didn't deserve to be shouted at, no matter how badly Dusty needed to shout at someone.

Working to keep his voice even, he asked, "Are the wedding guests gone? I've had about all the pretentious snobbery I can stomach for one day."

"They're gone, son," Max said in his gravelly voice, closing the carved oak door behind him.

"Thank heaven for that, anyway," Dusty muttered. When he'd learned of the theft last night, he'd been livid, and the silly pomp of his older brother's third wedding had hammered closed the lid on his ability to be civil. After maintaining a polite facade for as long as he could, he'd escaped to his den, thrown his tuxedo jacket and bow tie at the wall and wrenched open his ruffled shirt. He hoped this would be the last time one of Brett's brides required such high-toned baloney. This best man chore, done for a brother who was way too casual with relationships, was wearing thin.

Perturbed by Max's frown, Dusty turned his chair to face his desk again, placing his fists on the polished expanse. "What's wrong, then?" he demanded. "Is my brother's new wife already asking for alimony? That should be a record, even for him."

"No, Brett and Miss Patty—that is, Mrs. Dare—they're off."

A bitter chuckle rumbled in Dusty's chest. "Don't tempt me. I might have to agree." Noting his hired man's continued solemn expression, Dusty became guarded. "Okay, if the guests are gone and my brother and wife number three are off on their world tour, what's the problem? Is it Patty's daughter? Is she upset about having to stay here?"

"Miss Nicole's been looking a mite like a sparrow who can't find no worm hole, but right now she's gone off to take a swim." Max cleared his throat, his prominent Adam's apple bobbing the way it always did when the old man had to give his boss disagreeable news.

Apprehension tightened Dusty's gut. "What?" he growled. "Did you find something else missing? Damn Andrews! I trusted him, gave him a job. When I get my hands on him, I'll—"

"No, no," Max cautioned in a strained whisper. "No. It's . . . you have a visitor."

Dusty wondered why Max had hesitated; he was normally so hard to fluster. Yet as he stood there, shrunken and timeworn, his droopy gray eyes showed surprising distress.

"Who the devil is it?" Dustin cursed inwardly. What else could go wrong?

Not only was he CEO of Cherokee Natural Gas, which required him to oversee its burgeoning operation, he and Brett owned one of the most successful cutting-horse ranches in Oklahoma. And suddenly, thanks to Brett's honeymoon and Steve Andrews's thievery, Dusty had no managerial help for the stable. What now? he wondered again. By the look on Max's face, it would seem that someone with designs on his liver was standing outside.

Max's Adam's apple bobbed again as he whispered, "It's a female."

Dusty frowned. A female? What could be so bad about that? "And?" he prompted. "Is she wielding a chain saw and screaming, 'I want body parts'? If not, show her in."

Max motioned for Dusty to lower his voice again, admonishing, "Dusty, son, you don't understand. It's . . . it's a Miss Andrews. Anna Andrews."

"Andrews?" he echoed in a disbelieving roar. "Blast it! Andrews? Any relation to the sidewinder who stole from me?"

Max's expression grew more pained, and he lifted both gnarled hands in a plea for restraint. "Yes, she's the, er, sidewinder's younger sister, I'm afraid."

Dusty vaulted from his chair and stalked around his desk. "Well, don't keep her, Max. Send the lady in."

Shaking his head at his employer's show of anger, Max counseled, "She seems to be a sweet thing, Dusty, boy. Having 'bout as much fun as a baby with a bellyache. Don't bite the filly's head off. It's plain she's tryin' to help. 'Sides, her comin' here shows she's got a pile a grit in her gizzard."

"Maybe so," Dusty said, his tone grim. "But does she have a half-million-dollar Ross Sixkiller carving sticking out of her purse?"

Max shrugged helplessly. "Dusty. I'm asking you—don't chew her up and spit her out till you hear what she's got to say. Give me your word? She looks about as harmless as a newborn calf."

Dusty scowled at Max, his righteous anger rising to near-explosive levels. He cherished very few things the way he did the carving Steve Andrews had stolen—only his land and his horses were more valuable to him. This Anna Andrews had unknowingly arrived at a dangerous time, and from Max's worried expression, his deadly frame of mind was showing.

Poor Max. Over the years he'd broken up more than one fight between Dusty and some mouthy jackass. Usually it was after Dusty had been called something like "half-breed" or "wild savage." Even in Oklahoma Native Americans were in the minority, and there was always somebody who tried to feel superior by name-calling.

Dusty was proud of being half-Cherokee, and though his hot temper had nothing to do with being "wild" or Native

American, as a boy he'd always obliged a bully—no matter how big or tough—by jumping him and pounding him into the dirt.

One thing became apparent as the years passed—Dusty rarely lost when he was mad. Dustin Ross Dare was the fighter in the family, while Brett, it appeared, was the lover.

Three years older than Dusty, Brett hadn't cared much for the aggressiveness of the business world. He simply wanted to train cutting horses for competitions. But Dusty had never been able to do anything halfway. He was a mover, a shaker, a winner. He had to be the best at whatever he did, or he saw no reason for doing it at all. Six years ago, when he took over Cherokee Natural Gas after his father's death, he'd turned a local success into a sprawling giant, adding branches to the Tulsa firm that stretched from Louisiana to Utah. It had been the same way with Bent River Ranch. Despite Brett's laidback attitude, Dusty had molded the spread into one of the most highly regarded cutting-horse stables in the Midwest. First as a boy and now as a man, when Dusty fought, he won.

He was thirty-six, and he knew he shouldn't indulge in fistfights anymore, but there were moments when he had the urge. It wasn't because he'd been called a name, but it was still because of his Cherokee heritage. Part of it had been stolen with the carving, and that not only made him fighting mad, it hurt like the devil.

Exhaling what was very close to a curse, Dusty yielded slightly. "Don't worry, Max. I may be angry, but I don't beat up women. Send the lady in." The word "lady" had come out tinged with malice, and the sound made Dusty realize he'd have to control himself better. Anna Andrews was a thief's sister, but she didn't deserve to be convicted without a trial. Less sharply he said, "Tell Miss Andrews she can have five minutes."

ANNA HEARD the booming voice of an enraged man and fought the urge to bolt and run. She remained rooted to the floor, clasping her hands to keep them from shaking. The man had shouted the name "Andrews" as though it were evil, and she chewed her lower lip with renewed trepidation.

It was obvious Mr. Dare had been told who was waiting to see him, and she could tell by his snarl that he wasn't charmed by the idea. There was no way—no way on earth—he'd go for what she was about to suggest. She swept her fingers through her bangs, her hand shaking as if with palsy. She realized she was breathing heavily, too, and she'd gone all light-headed and dizzy. She just hoped she wouldn't fall into a dead faint at Mr. Dare's feet. Oh, why had Steven put her in such an unbearable position!

After her brother had left home, she and her uncle Bud found it difficult to get work training cutters. Some of the more honest ranchers admitted that they doubted a crippled old ex-cutting-horse champ and a petite inexperienced girl could adequately train their working stock.

For two long years Anna and Uncle Bud had struggled for every job, for every bite of food they'd put on the table, having to prove over and over that they were good at what they did—crippled and frail or young and small. They'd finally started to make some headway, since Anna had gotten older and progressively better as a trainer, but it was not exactly smooth sailing, especially with Steven's gambling.

Anna was tired of battling, and she'd had it with egocentric fireworks men. First her father and now Steven. They caused trouble everywhere they went, leaving deep emotional wounds along the way.

Anna hadn't slept well in ages, worried about her ailing uncle, their shoestring business and now this! Her brother was a fugitive from the law, forcing her to crawl and grovel and try to prove that the Andrewses were worthy of being trusted.

Here you go again, Anna! her mind nagged. *What if Mr. Dare is no different from the other ranchers? What if he tosses you out on your tail without giving you a chance?* "How," she cried softly to the empty echoing foyer, "could my own brother do this to me?"

She balled her hands into fists, swearing silently to heaven. *If one more of those hotheaded types gives me a hard time, I'll pound the stuffing out of him!*

Concentrating on breathing evenly, she chanted to herself, "Mr. Dare will be reasonable. He'll be reasonable. I'm here to help. I can help. He'll thank me. He'll be glad..." She only hoped she could convince herself before she faced the man whose shouts had so recently shattered the stillness of this big house.

Then Anna heard the elderly man's shuffling tread along the hallway to her left. She took a deep lungful of air to restore her determination and peered that way. His unhappy expression made her shiver. When he reached her, he said very solemnly, "Mr. Dare's willin' to see ya, miss." He gestured in the direction he'd come. "This way."

Resisting the urge to pull her lips between her teeth and gnaw on them, she nodded and moved down the hall, even though her mind was warning her that this was a crazy idea. Mr. Dare would never go for it.

She wondered for the thousandth time how her brother could have been so stupid, running off with the carving—in broad daylight, too. The lawyer had told her there was no doubt about his guilt. Several of the hired hands had seen him speed away, throwing gravel and burning rubber just before the theft had been discovered.

Anna was surprised Mr. Dare had had his lawyer call to give her brother a chance to return the carving before the police were notified. That had been more than fair. But try as she might, she hadn't been able to find Steven. And so, she was here, frightened out of her wits, to make a desperate appeal on Steven's behalf—to make a bargain if she could. Anna knew her proposal would sound absurd and that Mr. Dare would probably double over with laughter before bellowing a refusal. But that didn't matter. Her pride didn't matter. For Steven's sake, she had to make the attempt.

Standing before the imposing double doors to what she assumed was a den or an office, Anna watched as the old man opened one of the doors and stepped back, motioning her to enter. She smiled wanly and asked, "I have to walk the last mile alone?"

He smiled back, but it was a sad excuse for a pleasant expression. "Good luck, miss," he said, his tone gloomy, as though he'd said, "Rest in peace."

Nodding her thanks, she stepped into the lion's den. The door clicked shut behind her as her senses gathered up bits and pieces of information about her surroundings. Well-oiled oak paneling, the scent of leather, watercolors of quarter horses, furniture and draperies in shades of green, burnt umber and gold. On one wall a large glass-front display case brimmed with silver trophies. A colossal oak desk hunkered in the middle of the room.

Long arched windows at the far wall drank in gulps of June sunshine. Anna was surprised to see a crumpled gray jacket lying on the polished floor in a shaft of light. Her eyes followed the golden late-afternoon rays up and away from the jacket to fix on a motionless man standing, facing her, before one of the windows. She inhaled shakily at the vision he presented, for her silent adversary was massively tall and gilt-edged by the sun.

Although his features were obscured by shadow, Anna had no difficulty determining she was in the presence of a long-limbed male, elegantly clad and completely intimidating, if a bit rumpled. She felt out of place and shabby in her jeans and chambray shirt.

How was she to know that there would be a marriage ceremony taking place here today? The lawyer had never mentioned it, so she'd been forced to wait an uncomfortable hour outside the gate, at the insistence of the guard, until the guests poured out in a shiny slither of luxury cars.

Now, standing before Mr. Dare, she felt plain and unsophisticated. How could she convince him that she might be of any use to him at all? It was like trying to convince a lion that a mouse could be of service. Of course, that had been done once. Too bad it had been in a fable.

Through the dimness she could just detect a firm jaw that telegraphed a contrary streak, too. She sensed this was a person not easily dissuaded once his mind was set on a course of action—like sending her brother to jail.

"Well?" he asked without preamble, an ominous ring to the one-word question.

She swallowed, taking an unconscious step back. It took all her nerve to face his menacing presence with her head held high. "I . . ." she started, but her voice failed her. Her cheeks flooding with color, she began again. "I tried, Mr. Dare. I'm afraid I haven't been able to locate Steven."

"Damnation!" He ran an agitated hand through thick wavy hair that was the blue-black hue of Oklahoma crude. Then he said with a not-too-subtle threat in his voice, "You know what this means, Miss Andrews."

She barely nodded, barely breathed. "I... Yes. But I was hoping you'd agree to—"

"To what?" he cut in. "Making it an early Christmas bonus?" Contempt etched his words. "Dream on, lady. Do you have any idea how much a Ross Sixkiller carving is worth these days?"

Anna blanched. His lawyer had already told her the half-million-dollar market value of this particular carving: three wild horses caught in a racing, leaping tableau. The lawyer had also told Anna that the monetary loss wasn't the most important thing to Mr. Dare. Ross Sixkiller had been his grandmother's brother, and the piece had been carved to commemorate Dusty's birth. That had been before the Sixkiller pieces commanded the huge sums they did today. Even so, the lawyer had assured Anna that Mr. Dare was willing to forget the whole thing if the carving, *Windchaser,* was returned in the next twenty-four hours. And that deadline was fast closing in on her.

"Am I boring you, Miss Andrews?" came a gruff query, tearing Anna from her thoughts.

"Uh, no, I'm sorry…" She found herself twisting a strand of her long hair and immediately stopped, twining her fingers into a tight knot before her belt buckle.

"I trusted your brother, Miss Andrews, and he turned out to be a crook."

"My brother is not a crook, Mr. Dare. It's just that—"

"Forgive me," Dusty broke in, sarcastically. "I have a quirk about people who steal my possessions. Maybe I should get therapy."

She felt his ridicule like a slap. "Look, Mr. Dare," she said, trying to keep her courage from crumbling. "If you'd listen a minute, I'd like to help b-both you and my b-brother, that is…" She stuttered to a halt, staring. He was stalking forward in his anger, and his features were suddenly visible. Watching him come toward her was like watching someone rack a shell into a shotgun and take aim at your heart.

Dustin Dare's rough-hewn face, tanned by sun and wind, had a palpable impact on her senses. Within dark eyes the color of freshly turned earth, she saw a man ceaselessly driven, a man with fierce pride and little mercy. He exuded a fiery bearing and irrepressible hunger.

His lips, firm yet sensual, were drawn down in a frown, and the tense flexing of his jaw spoke of stubbornness and passion. There was a wildness about him that both beckoned and terrified her, a wildness that she hadn't detected when he'd stood farther away, backlit by the sun. But now it fairly shouted at her.

She scanned him from the muscular expanse of his chest in the half-buttoned shirt to the shiny cowboy boots he sported in spite of his otherwise formal attire. Dustin Dare obviously lived up to his name. He was a man of daring. A man never to be quite tamed, even disguised in the most elegant garments. As he drew nearer, the room filled with his energy. It pulsed and sizzled around her like a live electric wire—deadly to anyone who ventured to touch. She felt a warning throb deep in her soul. Before her was a man who never accepted second best, who could only be happy in competitive situations, a man who loved the chase but became bored once the capture was made. In other words, Dusty Dare was a fireworks man.

She wasn't very close to him, but she didn't have to be to know he was the essence of the volatile kind of male she'd vowed to avoid, and the knowledge made her grow sick inside. The last person she wanted to be around was someone like that. The last thing she needed was to be here, begging him to accept an offer that would require her continued presence. Still, if she was going to keep her brother out of jail, she had no choice.

He came to a halt barely a foot away from her, towering over her, powerful, commanding and devilishly handsome.

Something basic and female stirred inside her, and she was shocked at herself.

Fighting this wayward inner creature she'd never known existed, she surged on. "I hoped you would allow me to...to work for you as your stable manager. Let me temporarily take Steven's place. I thought you might give me thirty days while I try to get him to come back." She grabbed a quick breath, rushing on, praying he wouldn't end the interview abruptly by grabbing her by the scruff of her neck and tossing her out the window. "I...you see, my uncle and I, we've been running our business alone these past two years. Uncle Bud taught Steven and me a lot." Babbling from panic, she couldn't staunch the words once they began to pour out. "Our training stable isn't on this scale, but I'm good with horses—I've trained lots of cutters—and I thought I could help you out while I locate Steven. I'm sure if he knew of your kind, er, offer, he'd return the carving. I—" Her throat constricted at the frigid look that answered her proposal. She hadn't expected anything else, but she'd still hoped...

"Are you finished?" he asked.

She gathered her poise as best she could, considering his bothersome closeness and inevitable refusal, and nodded.

"You expect me to not only allow your brother to run around free for a month, but you want me to hire you, a pint-size woman who's trained...what? A few working cutters? And to manage my championship stables?"

The mocking incredulity in his voice made Anna flinch, but she'd come here expecting exactly this. Maybe not from a man quite so painfully handsome, but she had expected to be rejected—at first.

If the fire in his glare was supposed to make her give up and crawl away, then Mr. Dare was about to be hugely disappointed. What he didn't realize was that this pint-size woman had no plans to slink out with her tail between her legs. For her and her uncle to survive, she'd had to learn to shrug off rejection and charge ahead. "Yes," she said, braving his anger while trying to ignore the quiver in her limbs. "I believe you're a fair man," she told him, "and I believe if you wanted to press charges you would have done so last night. And...and I can do the work. You know Steven could, and we learned from the same teacher."

His gaze narrowed. "Are you crazy? You actually think I'll go for such a scheme?" He let out a disgusted laugh. "Do I look like Mother Teresa or a complete fool?"

She swallowed. He looked like the most deliciously assembled hunk of male ever created.

Her silence made him smile, but the expression wasn't friendly. "A fool, I gather," he muttered. "Don't count on it, Miss Andrews. I only gave your brother twenty-four hours because my lawyer thought it might convince him to return the carving, considering how hard it would be to find a buyer for such a well-known piece of art. Your brother isn't a very smart thief, I'm afraid."

"He was desperate!" she blurted. "And I don't think your lawyer suggested the twenty-four-hour limit at all. I think you make your own decisions, and I don't think you really want to send Steven to jail, or you would have reported the theft by now."

Dusty seemed surprised by her declaration, and his expression eased a little. For the first time Anna felt that he might be willing to listen, so she hurried on. "I've already called everybody Steve might contact and told them that you won't prosecute. As for my suitability for the job, well, even a pint-size woman is better than nothing. And you know it'll take you some time to locate a new trainer of the caliber you need." She decided to be completely truthful. "Besides, the guard at your front gate said your brother, who helps manage this place, will be gone a month. With both him and Steven gone—''

"Is that when you conjured up this infernal plan?" he broke in.

"It helped." She licked her lips nervously. "I really can train horses and manage a stable. My uncle's not in the best of health, and since Steven moved away, I've been doing most of the training, doctoring, handling of bills and such. I'd be working here strictly until you get permanent help, naturally."

"Naturally," he repeated, his lips twisting with scorn. "I'm afraid I'd have a hard time hiring another Andrews on anything but the most temporary basis."

"Then you'll do it?" she cried, fearful of believing her own ears. "You'll give me thirty days to get Steven to come back before you call the police, and you'll let me take over as—''

"Hellfire, Miss Andrews," he interrupted. "Hire the sister of a thief? You've got one sorry résumé."

"Fine," she shot back. "Rub salt in my wound if it makes you happy. But let's get one thing straight. I've taken all the insults I can stand from you. I've never done a dishonest thing in my life, and it hurts to be made to feel as if I'm the thief. I'm not, you know. I'm doing all I can to help, because I realize you're upset, and you have a right to be." Her voice broke. Humiliated that he had witnessed her weakness, she angrily continued, "If what I've suggested isn't good enough, say so and I'll leave, but I won't be yelled at one second longer." As she stared up into a face hardened by anger, her hopes died. She'd lost her temper. She never lost her temper. In her own defense, she wasn't used to being called a thief—or even the sister of one.

Anything she'd wished to accomplish here was beyond reach now. Resigned, she spun away, mumbling some inanity about not staying where she wasn't wanted, and hurried toward the door.

"What if he hasn't returned the carving at the end of thirty days, Miss Andrews?"

She halted, frowning, but didn't turn. "What?" she asked, not sure she'd heard his question right.

"I said," he began, nearer this time, "what if he hasn't returned my carving in thirty days? What then?"

She felt as insubstantial as morning mist. Could he really be considering her proposal? She twisted her head to peer into his unreadable brown eyes. Was he baiting her, or was he serious?

She hoped he was serious; his grave expression seemed to suggest that he was. "It won't come to that. I can't even consider it," she admitted at last.

Annoyance darkened his features. "I'm afraid I'm going to have to consider it."

She gaped, unable to speak. They both knew the ball was in his court now. All she could do was wait, listen and pray.

"If, at the end of thirty days, your brother hasn't returned my property, or it's damaged in any way," he said, his lips drawn down in a tight frown, "I will not only report him to the police and fire you, I will demand restitution from you to replace my loss. Are you willing to take that gamble for your brother's sake?"

The blood drained from her face. What was he saying? "You . . . you mean, if Steven doesn't return the carving, or if it gets broken or something, you'll take . . . take . . ." She couldn't go on. All they owned was a fifty-acre ranch and several thousand dollars' worth of livestock. The whole thing was worth only a fraction of his stolen carving.

"I'll take everything you've got," he finished for her. "At least everything up to half a million dollars. I wouldn't want to be accused of cheating you." He eyed her skeptically. "Do we have a deal?"

It was plain he expected her to back down. He didn't want her involved, didn't think the thirty days would make any difference as far as her brother was concerned. But she knew otherwise. She knew Steven wasn't really bad, just hotheaded. He'd come back as soon as he got word that Mr. Dare wasn't pressing charges. Making her decision, she said, "I have faith in Steven, Mr. Dare. I accept your deal."

He scowled, and she guessed he was disturbed that she would agree to such a one-sided bargain.

They stared at each other across a sudden ringing silence, and Anna was appalled to notice pity mingle with the contempt in his expression.

"He will be back, and I can handle the job," she insisted. "You'll see."

He looked away, and Anna saw a muscle flex along his jaw. He seemed to be trying to contain his frustration and was unwilling to say anything until he'd done so.

"I can start tomorrow. Where do I put my things?" she asked finally, if for no other reason than to dispel the awful stillness that hung in the room.

Plunging his hands into his trouser pockets, Dusty presented her with his back, muttering, "Hell!"

That hushed blasphemy was stark proof that, for as long as Steven and the carving were missing, Anna was going to have to cope with a rotten situation and an angry fireworks man! She exhaled slowly, silently, reining in her own emotions.

Honestly wanting to make everything work out, she offered, "I realize hell is where you'd like the entire Andrews family to go, but for now, where do you want me to put my things?"

He shifted to consider her over his shoulder. "Miss Andrews," he said tiredly, "if you're half as smart as that mouth of yours, you just might last out the week."

CHAPTER TWO

ANNA HAD JUST BEEN through the most stressful morning of her life. Not only had she worked like a dog since before dawn, she'd been scared out of her wits that the glowering Mr. Dare would show up and roar at her for not doing something properly. Each time his brutal handsome face came to her mind's eye, she doubled her efforts. Everything important depended on her staying here. Besides proving herself a good manager-trainer, she had to get the carving back, keep her brother out of jail and save her ranch. Thinking about it was enough to make her queasy.

The stable at Bent River Ranch was the biggest thing she'd ever seen, with twelve stalls on one side and a center aisle wide enough to drive a tractor through. Three oversize reinforced stalls to house stallions were located on the other side, along with five more regular stalls, a feed and tool room, a huge tack room, two foaling stalls and a paneled office. Behind the stable was a wash rack, a round training pen and the most modern indoor arena Anna had ever seen. This morning, as the tentative rays of a new sun began to wash the horizon in gold and pink, she'd feared the job might be too much for her, but she'd forced the notion from her mind. There was too much at stake to get fainthearted now.

After hours of hard work and worry, lunch wasn't going down well. Her stomach was tied in knots as she sat in the main house's big kitchen, picking at a cheese sandwich and half listening to Max while he rolled out dough for pies. He'd been telling her about his prize hybrid roses called red baubles or bubbles or something and a pruning technique he was particularly fond of. Apparently Max did more than the cooking around the place; he did the gardening, too. She tuned out, not hearing him, as she anxiously reviewed what she'd done so far today. Had she thought of absolutely everything?

She'd checked the forty quarter horses at five-thirty that morning. They'd all looked fit and healthy. Then she'd made sure Hunky, Flint and Ben, the hired hands, had fed and watered them, each according to the vet's instructions. She knew champion cutting horses were well cared for, but these animals had better medical care than most people.

The mares not to be worked today were led to the north pasture. While the hired hands mucked out the stables, she'd gone over the books, made a "to do" list, checked supplies and reviewed appointments noted on the calendar for next week. It appeared an interested buyer was coming over tomorrow to check out one of the more promising two-year-olds.

Anna took a sip of water, racking her brain. *What have I forgotten? Please let everything be all right!* She glanced up, something drawing her from her apprehensive meanderings. "What?" she asked Max.

"It's somebody on the phone for you, miss," he said, wiping his free hand on his makeshift dish-towel apron. "Wouldn't give his name."

Just then there was a clattering of sandaled feet at the door, and a teenage girl sprinted into the kitchen, holding a tall glass with melting ice in the bottom. "That my mom?" she almost pleaded.

Anna had seen the child moping around the place, and her heart had gone out to her. Nicole, yes, that was her name. Brett's new stepdaughter. Poor kid, Anna thought, all but deserted by her mother for a month, with only a scowling stepuncle and some servants for company.

"Sorry, little miss," Max said, holding the receiver toward Anna. "It's for Miss Anna here."

Nicole made a face and plopped into a chair, setting the glass down loudly. "Can I have more grape pop, Max?"

Curious as to who could be calling, Anna got up from the long pine table and took the receiver, thanking Max with a nod. "Hello?"

"Annie, kid?" came the whispered reply.

She knew immediately who the caller was. She'd have recognized her brother's voice anywhere. "Steven!" she cried, pulling inquiring glances from both Max and Nicole.

Lowering her voice, she turned away and whispered urgently, "Steven! Where are you? How could you have done such a terrible thing to Mr. Dare?"

"Look, Annie, kid," her brother interrupted. "I've only got a second. Just found out you were there and wanted to say I'm sorry for getting you in this fix, but it can't be helped. Got myself into some deep horse pucky this time, and I plan to dig me a hole and hide till I can pay those slime balls what I owe 'em. These guys play rough, and I don't wanna get my legs busted!"

"But, Steven," Anna pleaded, "that carving you stole won't do you any good. It's too well known to sell. Nobody will—"

"You let me worry 'bout that. Love ya, kid. Gotta go," Steve finished abruptly, then the line went dead.

She stood there staring at the receiver, tears welling in her eyes. Steven hadn't even given her time to tell him that Mr. Dare wouldn't press charges if he brought back the carving. If her brother had only given her a few more seconds...

"Don't tell me—that was your sticky-fingered brother."

Anna spun around. Nicole peeked tentatively out from behind Dusty's formidable torso. Anna caught her furtive movement and focused on the child, whose expression was wide-eyed and sheepish. It was clear she'd felt it her duty to scamper off to tell her uncle "the no-good thief," as Steven was being referred to around the Bent River Ranch, was on the phone.

Unfortunately for Anna, Dusty hadn't been far away. Probably eating lunch in the posh dining room, though his attire, snug jeans, green cotton shirt and roper boots, was far from posh. Nonetheless, Anna conceded inwardly, posh or not, he exuded virility and was an impressive male specimen.

"Do you speak English, Miss Andrews, or should I try my high-school Spanish?" he asked.

She came out of her stupor and blurted, "Oh, Mr. Dare, Steven, er...I tried, but I didn't have time..." Something in Anna's consciousness noticed that his hair drifted in lazy waves across his forehead and needed smoothing back. She floundered around to remember what she'd been saying. "And, uh, I'm..." She bit down hard on her lip. It seemed her mind had turned to mush. Privately she grumbled, *It's not all my fault. Your hateful expression would scare the wits out of savage thugs wielding automatic weapons!*

"Miss Andrews," he chided. "If you care for my horses the way you express yourself, I must assume they've all keeled over dead by now."

Her temper flashed, and she gave him a quelling glare. "I love horses," she said. "And I would do everything in my power to keep one of *them* from keeling over."

His eyes sparked at her unspoken implication. "I don't give a bent penny how you feel about me. As long as you do my horses no damage, you can stay on—for a time." With a quick jerk of his head, he ordered, "Let's go. I've got a couple of green-broke two-year-olds that need to learn some basics."

Her cheeks flamed. What he was asking her to do was so elementary it was embarrassing. A green-broke horse was one broken to the saddle, but just beginning its training with rein and knee signals. Not much challenge involved. Her boss obviously had no intention of allowing her to work with his prize horses, like Doc Hazard. The four-year-old chestnut stallion's dam was Doc's Sweetheart, who'd won the Futurity, the Derby and the Super Stakes—cutting's Triple Crown. He was sired by Hazard's Little Rio, also a cutting champion. And so, Doc Hazard was literally the best piece of horseflesh to come on the scene in years. Having already won the Texas Futurity this spring, he was a trainer's dream.

Swallowing the bile that rose in her throat, Anna challenged, "I thought I was here to train horses to cut cattle."

"You're here to do what I tell you to do, Miss Andrews," he warned as he descended the kitchen steps to the brick walkway. "Be grateful I'm not having you dig a manure pit."

"I thought you wanted Doc Hazard to get some heavy training in before competing again this fall. He'll need—"

"For the next thirty days, I'll train him—when I have time."

Dusty's tone told Anna that he didn't intend to debate the point. She was not to be trusted with his young champion.

Her boss's strides were long and deliberate, making it difficult for her to keep up. Quickening her step, Anna hurried toward his receding back. "Do you know who my uncle is?" she demanded, pride forcing her to go on in spite of his disapproving attitude. "He's Bud Sawyer. Does that name mean anything to you?"

"I know about your uncle. That he was one of the best trainers and competitors two decades ago, before that horse fell on him and crushed his legs."

"Well, then?" Anna said. "Don't you think I deserve a chance?"

He halted abruptly on the brick walk that curved along the manicured lawn toward the stables. Anna nearly collided with him. As he turned to confront her, she regained her balance and stared, fearful of what he was going to do.

"Miss Andrews," he said with deceptive calm, as though trying to reason with a half-wit, "my mother was a full-blooded Cherokee, and my father was part English and part Scottish. I have a relative in Scotland who's a member of the Queen's Highland Guard. However, that doesn't mean I can do the Highland fling."

He pivoted and headed away from her, never giving her a chance to respond. She was irritated by his impatient dismissal, something she should be used to by now, having been dismissed by so many potential clients over the past two years. But she wasn't used to it, darn it! She never would be. As a matter of fact, she was angrier than she'd ever been. Highland fling, indeed! His sarcasm hurt. "Why don't you give it a try?" she muttered under her breath. "Go Highland fling yourself off a cliff!"

He stopped briefly, which unnerved her. She had no way of telling if he'd heard her remark, for he said nothing, just resumed walking toward the stables.

Anna followed, fuming. Dusty Dare didn't intend to take her seriously. Well, she'd show him. She'd have the place ticking along like a thousand-dollar watch. And by heaven, she'd be on the back of Doc Hazard before the week was out. Mr. Dustin Dare would eat his doubting words.

Maybe Dusty Dare couldn't do the Highland fling, but Anna Andrews could cut a heifer out of a herd. Uncle Bud used to brag that she could turn a horse on a meat pie and never nick the crust. She was good! And she planned to show this man exactly how good—if for no other reason than the extremely galling fact that he thought she was worthless.

ANNA SAW Nicole Pratt again that afternoon. A pretty fifteen-year-old, she had long, straight black hair and deep blue eyes. Even though Anna had seen her only a couple of times, it was obvious that Nicole had a crush on Dusty. She tagged after him, wearing a moony expression that was so lovestruck it was comical.

Anna sat astride a two-year-old green-broke mare, teaching the rudiments of pushing signals from reins and legs. As she talked softly, soothing the horse, she used the reins to make small corrections to the animal's stance, to keep head, neck and shoulders aligned as needed for the mare to be guided through a new move.

From her vantage point, Anna watched with growing amusement as Nicole preened and simpered before her attractive stepuncle. Looking as though he was trying to ignore her, Dusty was cleaning Doc Hazard's hooves. Anna pretended to be absorbed in her duties, simpleminded though they were. She'd caught Dusty glancing her way a time or two, and his expression, though shadowed by the brim of his beige straw Stetson, was clearly one of sullen animosity, as if to say he was being bombarded from all directions by bothersome women.

"Uncle Dusty?" cooed Nicole, her lashes fluttering—a femme fatale in training. He grunted in response and lowered the stallion's foreleg, then stepped back to work on a hind leg.

"Uncle Dusty?" Nicole repeated, tugging on his sleeve. "I was wondering if you'd help me get a speck out of my eye." She paused as he continued to scrape the hoof, then added pitifully, "It hurts real bad."

Anna saw Dusty's hesitation, then watched as he lowered the horse's leg and straightened. "You wouldn't want these hands near your eyes," he said tersely. "They're filthy."

"Aw—" she sighed "—you've got real nice hands." Leaning forward, she poked out budding young breasts in a very unnecessary gesture for someone suffering from a speck in the eye. "I'm not worried." She lifted her face expectantly.

Anna had to press her lips together to keep from grinning. So, this tougher-than-nails man had puppy-love problems. She had to give her boss credit. He was trying to be a gentleman with his new niece, though the set of his jaw told Anna that he wanted to drop Nicole in a cold creek. Witnessing Dusty's struggle made Anna feel somewhat avenged for the rotten way he'd treated her since they'd met.

"I don't see anything, Nicole," Dusty said impatiently.

"Look closer," the teen coaxed, moving against him.

Dusty backed abruptly away. Then to Anna's surprise, he turned to give her a disgruntled look. "Miss Andrews?" he shouted. "Come here."

She dismounted and tethered her horse to the tie rail. "Yes?" She headed toward them, struggling to keep her expression passive.

Nicole looked at Anna, too, her expression a pout.

"What do you need, Mr. Dare?" Anna asked as innocently as she could manage.

Cocking his head toward the girl, he said, "She has something in her eye. Without my glasses, I can't see a thing."

"You don't wear glasses, Uncle Dusty!"

He turned back to his stallion and took up a hoof. "For that speck, I do," he grumbled.

"Okay, Nicole," Anna said, barely keeping a straight face. "Let's have a look."

The teen shook her head. "Nah, it's okay now." She shuffled off, plainly unhappy that she hadn't received more attention from the object of her affections.

Anna watched her go, then glanced at her boss as he reached out and stroked a scrap of red mane that dangled between the horse's keen bright eyes. Long tanned fingers moved gently and lovingly as he brushed the horse's forelock. For one crazy instant, Anna was envious of the animal and the casual intimacy it received from its master.

She was appalled to discover she'd been musing—no, more like indulging in romantic fantasies—about a man who was little more to her than a stranger, a stranger who didn't even like her. Troubled, she cast her gaze away.

The green-broke mare gave a high pitched nicker, and the soft innocent sound helped to gentle her ragged emotions. She glanced around and for the first time was struck by the beauty of the day. She'd been working so hard since she'd arrived, frightened by her boss's disapproval, that she hadn't allowed herself to notice. Bent River Ranch was enchanting—except for one troublesome man.

"Is there something else, Miss Andrews?" Dusty asked sternly.

She shrugged, wishing she really had this job, that she really belonged on this ranch—and that Dusty Dare lived somewhere else. Iceland seemed like a good place. "Not a thing," she retorted, trying to maintain a facade of disinterest. "And since the speck seems to be out of your niece's eye, I'll get back—"

"You and I both know there was no speck in that kid's eye!" he snapped. "I could see you out there barely able to keep from laughing."

She hadn't realized he'd noticed. The man was amazingly perceptive. Maybe that was part of the reason he was so successful. All she could do was shrug again. "Nicole's an impressionable girl who has, as I understand it from Max, lived in Tulsa in a condo all her life. You must be her first cowboy. Give her time. She'll get over her crush."

"I have a ranch and a business to run." He sounded exasperated. "Everywhere I've gone today, I've stumbled over her."

For some odd reason, Anna took pity on him. He did have a lot of responsibilities on his shoulders with his brother gone and his stable manager, er, gone, too. "She's just lonely and bored. I'll get her to do chores with me, if it'll help." She'd made the offer without conscious thought. When the words left her mouth, Dusty's startled expression couldn't have been much different from her own. But there was no backing out now. And in truth she didn't mind. She liked young people. Besides, if Nicole was going to live on a ranch, she might as well start learning about ranch life. Who better to teach her what a woman could do than another woman?

To Anna's surprise, instead of grinning and being grateful, Dusty's expression closed with skepticism. "I'd be crazy to allow that," he said, an edge to his voice. "You can't handle what you've got to do as it is."

She couldn't believe her ears. Incensed by his I-doubt-if-you-can-hack-the-job attitude, she met his skepticism with a jutted chin. "You're welcome. Think nothing of it. And just for the record, let me be the first to congratulate you on your absolutely terminal charm!" She whirled on her boot heel and headed back to her mare.

"By the way, Miss Andrews," he called, sounding un-bothered by her scorn, "exactly when did your brother say he'd return my carving?"

Dusty's reminder was like a dousing with ice water, and the heat of anger drained from her cheeks. Reluctantly she turned back. "I... He hung up before I had a chance to tell him about your offer." Trying not to allow his scowl to dismay her, she hurried on defensively, "But I have the word out, and I know it's only a matter of days, maybe hours, before he brings back your carving."

Dusty's legs were braced wide, one hand clutching the forgotten hoof pick, while the thumb of his other hand was looped behind his leather belt. His striking features were marred by severe doubt.

Unable to stand his censure an instant longer, she pivoted away and stalked out toward the mare, who was pawing the ground skittishly, as if sensing the tension that crackled in the air.

Ten minutes later, after successfully getting the mare to do her first tentative sidestep, Anna noticed Dusty leading his now-saddled stallion out of the stable. Dusty swung gracefully onto the horse's back, kneeing him into a gallop. A fine brown haze rose as man and mount headed off toward a lush pasture. It wasn't long before they'd disappeared into a thick stand of oak and pine.

Anna had no idea where they were going. Checking fences? Maybe cattle? Or simply heading out on a relaxing ride. She doubted that, though. Anna didn't think Dusty allowed himself to relax.

She shook her head. It wasn't hard to see why Nicole had a crush on him. Anna had made light of the fact that Dusty was probably Nicole's "first cowboy." No way was it that simple! With his muscular good looks, he was the essence of the legendary American cowboy—tall, ruggedly sexy—not to mention his Indian mystique!

Just now, with that Stetson pulled low on his brow, shadowing his features, he'd seemed to belong to the time when guns were worn low on the hip, and good men died on their feet. What girl—or woman—wouldn't experience a quickening of her pulse upon seeing that lean and lethal cowboy stalk in her direction?

She recalled his eyes, dusky and secretive one minute, flashing with fire the next. The vision haunted her, and she was finding it hard to ignore the attraction she felt. But she would ignore it, she vowed, because Dustin Dare not only disliked her and considered her a bottom-of-the-barrel, temporary hired hand, he was also a fireworks man. He'd never be happy with what he had, and his wife, if he ever married at all, would probably be a young beautiful trophy. No thanks!

As the day wore into evening, Dusty didn't return. Anna, Hunky, Ben and Flint groomed the horses and returned them to their stalls at feeding time. Nicole had been there, too, but she was frightened of the horses and whined more than she helped.

Finally, around seven, the day was over. Anna talked to the hands about what she wanted them to do the next morning, then made a list of things she needed to discuss with Mr. Dare. But with his continued absence, she was at a loss. While she ate dinner in the kitchen, Max went about his chores quietly and Nicole groused about hating horses and cows and ranch life in general.

"What if one of those big smelly beasts steps on my foot?" she whined. "I'll die and my mother will sue you."

Anna shook her head at the girl. "By the time your mother gets back, you'll be a regular Annie Oakley."

"Who?" Nicole asked.

"She's a famous cowgirl." Indicating Nicole's untouched plate of steak, carrots and hash browns, she said, "Now eat."

The girl made a face, but did as she was told, and the only sound was the clatter of dishes as Max filled the dishwasher.

Anna's dinner became a hard mass in her stomach. She needed to get away, take a ride. It was a lovely night, and an outing around the ranch would be calming.

Now that Nicole seemed engrossed in the meal, Anna gathered up her plate and ice-tea glass and asked Max, "Do you suppose Mr. Dare would mind if I went for a ride?"

He shook his gray head. "I s'pose your evenin's your own, miss. Still, can't figure why he ain't back." He took a scrubber and bent to work on an iron pot. "Dusty don't usually stay out ridin' this late, 'less he's riled 'bout somethin'."

Anna swallowed hard. He was riled, all right. With effort, she managed a smile. "Well, I guess I'll take a little turn around the ranch, then. See you in the morning."

"Do I have to wash your horse, too?" Nicole asked, a forkful of meat poised near her mouth.

Anna grinned at the girl. "No. The rule is, you ride it, you wash it."

"Good!" Poking the meat into her mouth, she mumbled, "I'm never gonna ride, then."

Anna managed a grin. "That's the old pioneering spirit," she teased, heading toward the back door.

"You need anything in your cottage, miss?" Max asked over his shoulder. "I can bring out some towels and the like."

Anna shook her head. "I'm fine. It's a lovely little place." At the kitchen door, she paused and turned back. "Actually, Max, there is something. When Mr. Dare gets back, would you tell him that I need to speak to him this evening?''

The cook nodded as he scrubbed. ''Sure thing, miss. But shoot, ya might meet up with him on the trail.''

Anna closed her eyes, disconcerted by the thought. ''I'd rather kiss a bug,'' she whispered gloomily, heading out into the moonlit night.

CHAPTER THREE

DUSTY LOUNGED on his back under an old pine, nibbling on a blade of grass, his head supported by his saddle and blanket. Staring up through the spiky boughs at the full yellow moon, he listened to the churning gurgle of the stream that danced and splashed only two feet away. The sound usually calmed his spirits on rotten days. But it wasn't working this time.

Hazard snorted restlessly and moved toward his reclining master to nudge him on the arm.

"Don't bother me," Dusty objected. "We'll go back when I'm ready."

He'd ridden out that afternoon, mad enough to eat the devil, horns and all. Steven Andrews's theft had come at the worst possible time. Dusty needed a good trainer now, more than ever. It was critical that Hazard's workouts be intensive. The Texas Futurity he'd won this spring was a prestigious victory, but for a prize stallion like Hazard, it was only the beginning. There would be some fierce competitions and millions in prize money ahead, and Hazard needed to be kept in top form.

But instead of an expert, Dusty was saddled with a fragile-looking woman whose main traits were youth and inexperience. She was probably twenty-four or -five, but she looked about eighteen. How could she expect to train a champion cutting horse, let alone run a stable as large as his? Her lack of experience in that alone would have been enough to make him double over laughing—if he hadn't been in such a serious bind.

He spat out the grass and hauled himself up, expelling a low-pitched oath. Hanging around out here, swearing in the dark, wasn't doing him any good. He might as well head back. And if he had any sense he'd fire Anna Andrews the minute he returned. But there was more than enough work to exhaust several men, and tomorrow being Monday, he had a full day of meetings at the Tulsa office. He supposed he'd hold off firing her for a while. She had a point—a minimal manager was better than no manager at all. He'd keep her on until he found a suitable replacement. That, unfortunately, might take some time.

After saddling Hazard, Dusty swung onto the horse's back and started along the moonlit trail toward the house. Holding the reins loosely, he allowed the stallion to have its head. Hazard knew the way and was eager to get back to his stall and his grain, leaving Dusty free to dwell on his problems. As he rode, he upbraided himself. What had possessed him to give Anna Andrews thirty days, anyway?

He frowned into the night as her face flashed in his mind. She had the same wide blue eyes as her no-good brother, though hers seemed to snap with an obstinate spirit and a passion for life that had been lacking in Steven's. Clenching his jaw tighter, he visualized her the way he'd seen her the first time. The woman had one heck of a lot of hair. When she'd come into his office, that long honey-brown stuff, which nearly reached her waist, had draped her shoulders like a silk shawl. He'd had a fierce urge to reach out and touch it.

Today he'd found himself strangely aware that she'd braided her hair exactly the way the tail of a cutter was braided for practice sessions to protect it from being damaged by the horse's own hooves.

Dusty snorted derisively at his wayward train of thought. To hell with Miss Andrews, her hair and her passion. The woman irritated him no end. She talked back, dared to suggest she knew what he was thinking, laughed openly at his troubles and practically demanded things go her way. She was the single most bothersome female he'd ever run across, and he'd bless the day she was out of his life.

After a minute he heard himself chuckle. To his surprise the sound held a trace of real amusement. "Terminal charm," he muttered, shaking his head. Why her insult struck him as funny he couldn't imagine. Maybe it was the way she'd stared daggers with those big, apprehensive eyes. She was an intriguing mix of pluck and panic. One minute he wanted to turn her over his knee, and the next he . . .

Dusty frowned as unexpected desire flowed through his body. Hell. He wasn't attracted to the woman. He didn't even like her. Both she and her brother were like burrs under his saddle. He supposed he'd felt a little sorry for her when she'd come by yesterday, twisting those slender hands together and looking serious and scared. She believed in Steven so much he hadn't been able to say no to her.

Hazard shifted nervously, capturing Dusty's attention. The stallion perked up his ears and came to a halt. Glancing quickly around to get his bearings, Dusty realized they'd reached the densest part of the woods. The moon's light was muted, almost nonexistent, beneath the lush canopy of leaves, and except for Dusty's light-colored hat, they were all but invisible in the darkness.

He was about to say something to soothe the animal when he heard it, too. Around a sharp bend in the trail he could hear the muffled hoofbeats of an approaching horse.

ANNA WAS RELIEVED to be out riding in the delicate June night. It was a pleasure and a luxury she would always cherish and hoped never to have to give up. If only her ex-fiancé, Thad, had understood her love for the wide open spaces and the company of a good horse. Thad was such a hardworking, solid person. It was too bad he was unable to see her side of this one important issue. With a wistful sigh, she put thoughts of Thad aside and gave herself fully to the freedom of the nighttime excursion.

All the stress of the day had seemed to melt away the instant she'd left the stable area and galloped across the moon-burnished pasture. The dapple-gray Anna had chosen for her ride was a mare named Candy Cane. She was a good cow horse, but no champion. At first, she'd found the little mare inordinately stubborn about accepting the bit and being led out of her stall, but now, her mount seemed to be enjoying the outing.

The woods had grown progressively thicker and darker as they'd ridden, and Candy had slowed to a walk. The coolness of the thicket and the rustling thrumming sounds quickened Anna's senses. She smiled, inhaling the tart pungency of the forest.

Without warning, Candy shied to the right, startling Anna. Seasoned horsewoman that she was, she wasn't unseated by the mare's unexpected skittishness. As Anna gentled her with a soft word, she glanced up and was confronted with the reason for Candy's distress. Rounding a bend in the trail, making hardly a sound, came a horse and rider. The man's hat, almost luminescent in the moonlight, was pulled low over his face. Yet there was enough illumination for Anna to discern a sweeping expanse of shoulders and well-muscled body moving in the saddle with an all-too-familiar grace.

Forbidding as doom itself, he reined his mount to a halt, saying nothing. An echoing stillness surrounded them for what seemed like an eternity before Dusty finally demanded, "What in blazes are you doing out here?"

Candy Cane sidestepped, uneasy, and Anna couldn't blame the mare. Mr. Dare and his big stallion materializing out of nowhere like that had been startling, to say the least. But she refused to allow him to intimidate her. In her most businesslike tone, she ventured, "Oh, hello, Mr. Dare. This is a coincidence."

The stallion snorted.

Dusty laughed curtly. "My sentiments exactly, Hazard." When he shifted forward in his saddle, his manner grew slightly threatening. "Who gave you permission to take out one of my horses, Miss Andrews?"

She was affronted. "I thought, as stable manager, I could exercise a horse if—"

"Forget it," he cut in. "To tell the truth, I don't give a plug nickel, right now. It doesn't matter so much with Candy Cane, anyway." He shifted back in his saddle, and there was a squeak of leather. "That mare's so barn sour I can't figure how you got her to leave the barn at all."

Insulted, Anna grumbled, "I can't figure that, either, since I'm such a lousy horsewoman."

He cocked his head. After a minute and without another word, he signaled his mount forward. When he passed her on the trail, their legs brushed, and Anna felt a shiver course through her body. She must have telegraphed her reaction to Candy Cane, for the mare grew goosey, prancing sideways and pawing the earth.

It was all Anna could do to calm her mount and breathe at the same time. Dusty's insolent presence had an odd way of short-circuiting her competence, both at being an effective rider and a rational woman.

"One more thing, Miss Andrews," Dusty called back, causing Anna to stiffen reflexively.

She couldn't bring herself to turn around, but decided he probably couldn't tell in the dark, anyway. "Yes, Mr. Dare?" She forced her voice to be as firm as his.

"I want you in my office in forty minutes."

She swallowed. So much for a stress-free ride. "Yes, Mr. Dare," she responded, fighting her disappointment. Then patting Candy Cane's neck, she whispered, "Soon, honey. We'll do this again, soon."

Anna shivered with trepidation, praying this upcoming meeting wouldn't be the one in which Dusty would tell her he'd changed his mind and had decided to fire her.

Reining her mount around, she was stabbed by guilt, wishing she hadn't made the little mare promises she wouldn't be able to keep.

ANNA DIDN'T HAVE to knock. The door to Dusty's office was swung wide, giving her a clear view of him, his booted feet propped on his desk and his masculine torso sprawled negligently along the length of his leather chair.

He'd been going over some papers when she'd come in, but apparently she made a sound, for his glance shifted in her direction. He surveyed her for a moment before his lips curved in a mocking half smile. "Just how old are you, Miss Andrews?" he queried. "You look like a teenage wallflower at a 4-H Club dance."

Anna stifled the urge to tell him his rudeness was almost as offensive as his raging ego. She sensed he was trying to get her so mad she'd quit this job. Well, he'd have a long wait. She had no intention of doing his dirty work for him. After counting silently to ten, she said, "I suppose, as my employer, you have a right to ask a few personal questions. I'm not sure that's one of them, but I'm not ashamed of my age. I'm twenty-six."

A dark brow lifted in what appeared to be disbelief. "Miss Andrews," he said with an almost imperceptible nod toward a chair, "sit down."

Her glance fell to the spot he'd indicated. The carved and padded antique was a rather spindly excuse for a place to sit, but Anna figured it must be an expensive family relic. Resisting the urge to dust off her jeans, she walked to the chair and perched on it. She knew she looked about as relaxed as a horse with three legs off a cliff, but she was doing the best she could under the circumstances. This man held her family's fate in his hands. "Yes, sir?" she managed.

He placed the papers he'd been perusing next to his hat on the desk. Lowering his feet to the floor, he stretched, then leaned back in his chair. "Max tells me you wanted to talk to me?"

His statement startled her. "I... Yes, but I thought you wanted to..." The sentence died away. *Why remind him!* she scolded herself.

Dusty nodded. "I did, but why don't you go first."

His expression was speculative, and Anna had the feeling he was about to give her an oral exam. If so, then it was still possible she might pass his test. He might not be bent on firing her, after all. Clinging to that possibility, she cleared her throat. "I did want to discuss a few things..." She hesitated a moment, then went on, hoping he hadn't noticed, "It concerns the horses' care. I checked the supplies, and we're in pretty good shape for the most part. One thing, though, I noticed in the records that it's time for the horses to have their booster shots. I have plenty of experience giving them. But when I looked through the medical supplies I discovered we're low on the one-and-a-half-inch twenty-gauge needles."

When she paused for air, he merely nodded, and she decided he meant for her to go on. "I see by Steven's—" she faltered briefly when she noted his grimace of irritation at the mention of her brother's name ''—planner that your three-year-old, Lady Freckle Handy, is to be worked with cattle three times a week to get her ready for some cutting competitions this summer. I've taken a look at her, and she's athletic enough. Is she pretty cowy?'' she asked, referring to a horse's natural desire to control cattle.

He frowned, as if the question had been absurd, as if any of his prize horses could be anything else! ''She has a tendency to charge the cow, if anything,'' he said. ''That's why I want her in some small-purse competitions this summer. To help break her of that. She's got championship potential. The first time we had her in with cattle, she put her head down and went nose to nose. With training, she's going to be a big money winner.''

''You're taking her slower than Hazard to avoid burnout, I gather.''

At the mention of his prize stallion, Dusty flashed an extraordinary smile. Anna knew the expression had nothing to do with her remark, but was an unconscious show of pride for the animal. With a chuckle, he said, ''Hazard'll never burn out. For fun, that damn horse was cutting the family dogs when he was a colt. Drove them crazy. He's perfect. Aim him at a cow and you can throw your reins away, 'cause he takes over. Lord, I love that horse. He's like me. Lives for a challenge.''

Anna felt an unsettling thrill dance along her spine. She'd never seen such passion in this man before, never even seen a genuine smile on his face, and the sight was frighteningly beautiful. Too bad he'd just reinforced what she'd already determined about him—that he was recklessly bold, exactly the type of man her mother had always warned her about.

But there was something else she realized when she looked into his smiling face. He might love to win, might be breeding his horses to be champions. But he loved them, too. That was a point in his favor—amid a whole pile of points against.

Dusty sobered, inspecting her strangely. She wondered what her face was registering, but before she could react, he steered them back to the subject. "What were you saying about Freckle?"

Anna gripped her hands in her lap. *Here goes.* "Well, I have an idea that I think would help fine-tune her moves. And if you like the way she responds, I thought, er, you might want me to work Hazard with them, too."

He peered at her narrowly. "Them?"

A wave of apprehension swept through her, but she believed in what she was about to suggest. This training method had worked for Uncle Bud, and it had worked for both her and Steven in training horses for area ranchers. Lots of smaller spreads with limited budgets trained cutting horses this way. Even some of the bigger operations were starting to try it. Facing him squarely, she steadied herself and murmured, "Goats, Mr. Dare. I'm suggesting we work Freckle with goats once a week."

He inclined his head, looking as if he wasn't sure he'd heard her right. "What did you say?"

Uneasy beneath his watchful scrutiny, she fidgeted, squeezing the scrawny arms of her chair. "Uh, goats..."

She was sure he heard her that time. There was a distinct hardening in his eyes. "Goats?" he repeated, his tone critical and vaguely amused.

"I...I know it's considered kind of a maverick idea to most of the bigger spreads, but the practice is catching on. Goats are faster than cattle, and cutting them takes more quickness and cow sense than—"

"Miss Andrews," he interrupted, "you don't need to tell me about training cutting horses with goats. I don't live on Mars. But in my opinion we don't need to go to that extreme. I have five hundred excellent Herefords that are here specifically for the purpose of fine-tuning my horses. I don't intend to start a goat herd, too."

"Uncle Bud and I have goats," she offered quietly.

Dusty sat forward, his vexation evident. "I'm happy for you, Miss Andrews. However, that doesn't affect my decision. No goats."

"You'd be surprised at how well they work," she went on, refusing to be bullied.

"If it's so great, why didn't your brother bring it up?" Dusty challenged, pushing himself out of his chair.

"Steve is a people-pleaser, Mr. Dare. I guess he figured you'd react this way, and he didn't want to make you mad."

Dusty's laugh was short and humorless. "So he decided to please me by stealing from me. I'll have to thank him."

His remark hurt, but Anna didn't have a retort. Steven had done a terrible thing and there was no defending him.

Dusty came around his desk, halting a scant foot from her chair to glare at her. "Apparently you and your brother don't share that particular trait."

She was confused, and his nearness didn't help to clear her mind. "What trait?"

"The people-pleasing one." His smile was unpleasant. "It would be a nice change, Miss Andrews, if you made an effort to please me, since I *am* your employer."

"I'm doing my best," she countered through clenched teeth. "I can't help it if you refuse to see that."

She noticed that the muscle in his jaw had begun to bunch and jump, so she prudently cast her gaze down, worrying that he'd had about enough. Maybe she'd gone too far. But if he wasn't so bullheaded . . .

"Miss Andrews," he growled, "the reason I called you in here tonight was to fire you."

She jerked up her head to stare at him. She *had* gone too far! In some sort of cruel mental movie, she watched everything she loved being taken away—Steven being marched off to jail, her ranch being confiscated by Mr. Dare's lawyers, while she, Uncle Bud and their thirty-two hungry goats sat by the side of a lonely dirt road with no place to go.

"But I've changed my mind—for now," he said, giving her a disgruntled look. "Go ahead with the inoculations."

Anna squinted, uncomprehending, as though he was speaking a foreign language. She had no time to ask what he meant, for he was still talking. "And get what supplies you feel we need. Also, I'll think about allowing you to work with Freckle. As for Hazard, that's out of the question. As for the rest—" he paused, pursing his lips for a moment as though in troubled thought "—keep doing what you did today. You can be sure I'll watch your progress, and we'll talk again later in the week when I have time."

He folded his arms across his chest, the move a wordless indication that the interview was over. Somewhat feebly, she managed to get to her feet. Not only was she still working as Bent River Ranch's manager-trainer, but she had been given quite a bit more responsibility than she'd expected!

Nodding, she mumbled, "Thank you, Mr. Dare..." The words came out tense, in spite of her numbness.

His brows dipped as though he guessed she'd like to argue a point. It amazed her that he had such an insightful nature. She did want to discuss one thing, though—his lack of wisdom about keeping Freckle and Hazard inactive when both the stallion and the mare needed challenging workouts.

"Well, what in blazes is it?"

His scowl made her want to leave the room at a run, but she knew, for Hazard's sake, she must speak up. "It's just that, er, Uncle Bud always gave me the stallions to train, Mr. Dare. He said stallions respond to women better because there isn't that male-ego clash. I mean . . ." She rushed her words when he looked like objecting. "You see, a stallion is strong-willed and so are most men."

"You're going to tell me about men, now?"

"No, don't be silly," she shot back, then caught herself, composing her face and her voice. "What I mean is, a woman is more nurturing. I've always handled stallions well."

"Miss Andrews," he began, clearly trying to control himself, "Hazard is very possibly the finest cutting horse on the face of this planet. Only an expert with years of experience could walk the line between pushing him too hard, taking the 'cow' out of him, or being so easy that the head-strong element you're talking about would take over and he'd become too aggressive." With both scorn and pity in his tone, he told her, "The hard truth is, you don't have the age or experience to have the ability to walk that line. You may be pretty good, but this is a future world champion we're talking about, not some cowboy's weekend hobby. As I said, I may allow you to work with Freckle—in another week or so. Most trainers would kiss my feet for being allowed to do that!"

She stood rooted there, inches from him, frozen with annoyance. "I've only been trying to convince you that I can help," she said stormily, "and that I know what I'm doing—" She cut herself off as his lips thinned in displeasure. What good would ranting and raving do? He wasn't listening. Straightening herself to her full five feet five inches, she managed thickly, "Is that all, sir?"

His nod was curt and his stare so cold it could have chilled a side of beef. "Good night, Miss Andrews."

Thoroughly dismissed, she headed for the door.

Before she stepped across the threshold, he called, "If you know what's good for you, no more talk about trucking in any of your billy goats."

Barely able to contain her resentment, she barreled through the exit, muttering, "Why not? Why should you be the only contrary buck on the place?"

"I didn't catch that," he said. "Was it something about my terminal charm?"

There was too much mockery in his tone for Anna to attempt an answer. He would definitely fire her if she told him the uncharitable things she was thinking.

In a desperate bid to keep from losing everything she'd just gained because of one hot-headed urge to talk back, Anna rushed along the hall at a breakneck pace. She craved nothing more than to put acres and acres of distance—no, make that continents and continents—between herself and that arrogant tyrant!

CHAPTER FOUR

THE DAY WAS SO BEAUTIFUL Anna had taken her work out onto the veranda attached to her office in the stable. Now that she'd done the necessary inoculations, she was updating the health records. The June afternoon was laying a warm hand against her face, as the sun, dropping toward the horizon, furtively slid its rays beneath the wide veranda's covered roof. The breeze was sweet with the smell of wildflowers mingling with the tart aroma of horses and hay. She smiled, looking out over the rolling green landscape, crisscrossed with white wooden fences marking off pastures and training paddocks that went all the way to the edge of the woods.

Heavens! she mused. This ranch was a perfect place for anyone who loved horses—a trainer's dream. She sobered at the thought, wondering for the thousandth time how Steven could have been so foolish to throw away such a great opportunity.

The breeze fluttered her page, and she smoothed it down, carefully printing the dosage of influenza vaccine she'd given Freckle, along with today's date. "There." She closed the book, satisfied that the inoculations had gone well. "Find fault with that, Mr. Dare," she muttered, standing up.

When she reentered her wood-paneled office, she thought she heard her name being called. Replacing the record book in its niche on the shelf behind her desk, she went to her office door and listened.

"Anna?" came a distant call.

She recognized the voice, now. It belonged to Thad, her ex-fiancé. It had been a month since they'd broken up, and she hadn't heard a word from him in all that time. What in the world was he doing here?

Stepping into the wide central aisle, she saw a slender man slightly under six feet tall, standing beneath the vented cupola in the stable's center. Her eyes widened at the sight of him. He wasn't dressed in his usual three-piece suit and silk tie. Instead, he was wearing cowboy apparel from the top of his white ten-gallon hat to the tip of his needle-toed boots.

He wore a red-and-white checked shirt reminiscent of a pizza-parlor tablecloth, a bolo tie, a big silver belt buckle in the shape of a truck and white designer jeans. She was so appalled at his idea of what a cowboy was supposed to wear, she could only gape. "What's...what's all this?" she asked finally, spreading her arms to indicate his gaudy attire.

He was grinning broadly. "Howdy, ma'am." He tipped his hat to show off his blond curls, then plopped the monstrosity back on his head. "I was just promenadin' through this burg and thought I'd mosey over to see y'all."

Anna was confused. Hadn't she and Thad decided their wants and needs were just too different for them to ever make it as a couple? She loved horses, and he was allergic to hay dust. She craved a solid permanent home, and he managed a hotel and could be transferred any time. She loved the wide open spaces and any wife of his would have to live in a hotel suite in town. Hadn't they reluctantly decided all that was too much to overcome? If so, what was this?

"Why are you so dressed up, Thad?" she asked. "Are the Village People making a comeback?"

Thad's grin faded slightly. "What? Is there something wrong with my duds?"

She shook her head at him. "Let's just say, if you ever decide to wear that to an actual rodeo, I'd suggest one more accessory?"

"What's that?"

"A big gun." She walked over and smiled. She thought Thad was the most stable hardworking man she knew, and she respected him for that. It wasn't his fault they were so different. "Where did you buy that stuff—Tenderfeet-R-Us?"

His expression was suddenly downcast. "Well, heck, I tried. Don't I get points for that?"

She frowned, completely baffled. "Points? For what?"

His smile returned. "Anna, sweetie, I've got a surprise for you. I've saved up a week's vacation, and I've decided to spend it with you. Here! Learning to be a cowpoke!"

She stared at him, not believing her ears. "You... you want to..."

He nodded vigorously, his grin as bright as ever. "Yes— I mean, yup! I want to understand what it is that you love about this horse stuff." He gestured expansively, then sneezed, shuddering from head to foot, then sneezed again as he dragged out a handkerchief to stifle a third. When he'd composed himself, he wiped his watering eyes and stuffed the kerchief into his hip pocket. "I want to be your John Wayne."

She knew her expression must be pained, but she couldn't help it. "This is crazy, Thad. You can't even breathe out here."

He waved his hands before him, negating that suggestion. "New medication's going to handle that. I'm picking it up this afternoon." He pulled her into his arms for a quick kiss, murmuring, "Tomorrow, you teach me to ride."

"Tomorrow? You mean here? Tomorrow?"

He nodded. "Sure. Why not?"

"But, Thad, Mr. Dare won't allow that. I've got work to do."

"I'll help you work. Then on your breaks you can teach me to ride."

"On my breaks?" she echoed, doubtful. "Thad, this isn't a nine-to-five thing with a morning and afternoon break, an hour for lunch, then dashing off the minute the whistle blows."

He shrugged nonchalantly. "Okay, whatever. But I'm here to lend a hand and . . . and . . ." He sneezed again.

"And blow your brains out, it sounds like."

"I told you, I'm picking up the hay-dust prescription today. I'll be a new man in the morning. Wait and see."

"Wow!" came a young voice. "Killer jeans."

Nicole ambled out of the tack room on Anna's right. She was carrying a kitten. She'd discovered one of the three barn cats had had a litter in a drawer there, and she was delighted.

"Nicole," said Anna, "this is Thad Kelly, my—a friend of mine."

Nicole smiled at Thad and nuzzled the purring ball of gray-and-white fuzz. "Hi, Thad." She walked around to critically eye the hip pocket of his jeans. "Monsieur Aphrodite's a dynamite brand."

Thad winked at the girl. "Now there's a woman with taste." He nodded benevolently. "Well, sweetie, I've got to get back and pick up the medicine. What time should I be here tomorrow?"

"Uh, Thad, really, this isn't a good time. I've been pretty busy." She tucked a loose strand of hair behind her ear. "This place is so big I've been swamped with work. Besides, Mr. Dare is barely tolerating me as it is. I just don't think he'd go for—"

"Well," Thad interrupted, "you tell him you have a free hired hand for a week and see how upset he gets. He's a businessman—he'll be glad I've offered my services." He rubbed his thumb against her chin in an affectionate gesture. "Honestly, Anna. I've missed you. I want to get back into your good graces. Let me do this for you—for us both."

She had a sinking feeling in her stomach. Apparently he'd thought about their relationship during this past month and decided he didn't want it to end. She had to admit she'd been unhappy about having Thad out of her life, too. Hadn't her mother always said, "Find a solid hardworking man, Anna. If love isn't there at the beginning, it will come. Respect each other, care for each other. That's what counts." Her mother had loved her father, Abe, wildly, unreservedly. But he'd loved action, adventure and challenges more than anything else. Finally he'd left when life with his wife and two young kids had become a bore. Three years later, Bruce, Anna's stepfather, had come along. He was a little dull, but steadfast. Over the years, her mother had been content.

She stared into Thad's pea-green eyes, so earnest, almost pleading, and she couldn't say no. With a sigh, she nodded. "My day starts about five, but you don't have to get here that early."

He laughed out loud and hugged her to him. "Sweetie, I'll be here at five. Love you." With that, he swept off his big white hat and left, bellowing, "Yahoo!"

When he was gone, Nicole said, "That's your boyfriend, isn't it?"

Anna shrugged. "He was once."

"Kind of a geek, but he's nice. And he sure has got the hots for you."

Anna gave Nicole a startled look. "The hots? What do you know about such things?"

Nicole laughed. "I'm fifteen."

She said "fifteen" as though it meant the same thing as "Wake up and smell the coffee!" Anna decided not to pursue the subject.

Nicole was cradling the kitten and looking like a little girl. Anna wondered if fifteen-year-old girls had it harder now than she'd had it. Did they know too much, or had she known too little?

"Do you think Scumface can stay in my room?" Nicole asked, drawing Anna from her musings.

"Scumface?" she asked. "I can't imagine why you'd want to take someone with such a horrible name to your room."

Nicole held up the kitten, kissing its nose. "This is Scumface. Isn't he sweet? I named him after the lead singer in my favorite grunge group, Spit on My Shoes. It's a totally killer band."

Anna nodded, hoping her horror didn't show. "I see. Well, you'll have to ask your uncle Dusty about Scumface. It's his house. Meanwhile, I have a feeling the tack room still needs to be swept."

"Aw, now?" Nicole whined, kicking at a pile of straw with her chunky combat-style boots. "My fave soap's about to come on."

"Tape it, put Scumbag back with his mother and get the broom."

"You're mean, Anna. Almost as mean as Uncle Dusty. And it's Scumface not Scumbag!"

Anna felt badly, not because she was making the girl do some light chores, but because Nicole had chosen to compare her to the grouchy Mr. Dare. "Whatever," she said, swiveling to return to her own work. She stopped when she realized that Mr. Grouchy himself was standing close by, glowering in her direction.

"Uh, is there something I can do for you?" she asked.

His glower moved from her to his niece. "No," he muttered, moving past Anna with hardly a glance. "Nicole?" he said.

Anna knew it wasn't her business, but she couldn't just leave. Poor kid. What was he going to growl about now?

Anna watched Nicole's features pinken. A mixture of puppy love and apprehension was starkly evident on her face. "Yes, Uncle Dusty?" she whispered, clutching the kitten to her breast.

He surprised Anna by kneeling before the girl and reaching out to stroke the kitten. "How's it going?"

Nicole swallowed. "Fine . . . sir."

"You like the kitten?" he asked, lowering his hand to his knee.

Nicole nodded. "I . . . I never had a pet before. I was sort of wondering, maybe . . . maybe . . . that is, Anna said I should talk to you. I . . ." The words slid away into nothingness, and Nicole blushed furiously, no doubt too frightened of his rejection to go on.

Anna bit her lip, feeling for the girl, but she didn't say anything.

"You want to keep the kitten in your room?" Dusty guessed. Or had he overheard Nicole a minute ago? Anna didn't know.

Nicole nodded, her eyes filling with tears.

Dusty frowned and looked away. He appeared to be thinking about it. After a moment, he said, "I tell you what, Nicole. Go have Max put kitty litter on his shopping list. As soon as he gets it, the kitten can stay in your room."

Both Anna and Nicole let out a gasp. Anna's was obscured by Nicole's, which was loud enough to startle several mares. They nickered and whinnied in agitation.

With happy enthusiasm, Nicole hugged her uncle, crying, "Oh, thank you, Uncle Dusty. I love you! And I love Scumface." Smacking a sloppy kiss on Dusty's cheek, she dashed off into the tack room.

After the teen had gone, Dusty stood and turned to go, but stopped when he saw that Anna was still there. Lifting a questioning brow, he asked, "Did you need something?"

She shook her head, but couldn't suppress a small smile. "That was nice of you. Why did you let her have that kitten?"

He leaned against a stall support, eyeing her solemnly. "Until I overheard her call me mean, I had no idea I'd been so hard on her. I guess I've been so busy I haven't thought of her feelings." He lifted a shoulder casually. "And since Patty didn't leave her daughter here to be bullied, I figured I owed her something. The kitten seemed little enough."

Anna felt herself soften toward her boss and allowed herself to admit it. "It's the kindest thing I've seen you do. But I'm afraid it won't help ease the crush she has on you."

He shook his head dismissively. "I think you're making too much of that."

"Maybe," she said, doubtfully. Then it occurred to her she should mention Thad's bombshell about coming to the ranch. "Oh, by the way, Mr. Dare?" He halted just as he'd begun to amble away. "Thad Kelly, my ex—er...an old friend is going to be dropping by during the next week. To...help out," she hedged, deciding her boss didn't have to know about the riding lessons. She'd manage to give them to Thad somehow, without interfering with her job.

Dusty's eyes narrowed a fraction. "Oh? What did you say he was? An ex-something? I hope it's ex-championship trainer, but the name isn't familiar."

Anna's face went hot with embarrassment. "No. Thad can't actually even ride, but he's willing to—"

"Willing to what?" He silenced her, his tone mocking. "Hell, Miss Andrews, this isn't 'The Dating Game.' It's a business. I don't want any screwing around on my time. Is that clear?"

She bristled at his bluntness. "Congratulations. That is by far the crudest remark anyone has ever made to me! For one second, wrestle your mind out of the gutter and re- member this—I'm doing everything humanly possible to make amends for what Steven did." She ignored him when he tried to interrupt. "Okay, so maybe Thad picked a bad time to try to get back together with me, but if he's willing to help along the way, you should be happy. I know you're upset about what my brother did, but to be frank, you've been about as nice to me as a dentist's drill. Couldn't you at least be civil?"

He met her angry glare and held it. The seconds passed slowly, agonizingly. "I'll think about it, Miss Andrews," he finally said, his tone grim. Shifting around to give the horses in the nearby stalls a cursory look, he asked, "How did the inoculations go?"

"Fine!" she snapped. "I'm happy to report only six dropped dead."

He examined her with hooded eyes. "Be in my office at ten tonight." His fierce tone knotted her stomach with foreboding. It was as plain as the sun at high noon she'd crossed that line again. And tonight he was going to make her pay.

WITH THE DAY'S WORK completed, dinner over and her nerves frayed, Anna took Candy Cane out for a long calming ride. At least it was supposed to be calming. It wasn't. She was still anxious and miserable when she returned to the stables.

Once she'd used up as much time and nervous energy as she could grooming Candy, she returned the mare to her stall, then roamed aimlessly across the manicured back lawn of the ranch house, her hands fisted in her jeans pockets, her jaws clenched with dread.

Ten o'clock! Why such a late meeting? Why draw out her torment that long? It was only nine. Time seemed to be dragging by with the sole purpose of torturing her. Some incessant gremlin in her brain nagged and nagged about the looming meeting with Mr. Dare. He wasn't about to let her insolence go unnoticed. She didn't know what to do. Fall to her knees and beg for mercy? Or simply take her punishment and go?

Maybe if she told him the truth—that she was so terribly worried. And because of her agitated state, she said things she didn't mean. Surely he knew she was half out of her mind with fears about Steven! And for some demented reason, Dusty Dare unsettled her so badly she said things she would never say, never *had* said, to another soul on earth!

She chewed her lower lip, uneasy about her mixed feelings for him. There was such boldness hovering in his eyes, such tremendous male grace in the way he moved. He was exciting to be near, even when he growled at her.

So, in her attempts to fight her attraction, she blew every conversation with him by snapping and talking back. No wonder he was angry with her.

She made up her mind. She'd plead for a second chance. Steven's freedom and her family ranch depended on her being civil to Mr. Dare. From now on, no matter how nervous and flustered and upset his scowling presence made her, she'd bite her tongue and say, "Yes, sir!" Even, "Yes, Your Majesty," if he insisted. Whatever he wanted, he'd get. She'd turn over a new leaf. Be meek and obliging.

Anna caught a movement out of the corner of her eye and peered into the distance. About fifty feet to her left, up a slight rise, was the pool, surrounded by a privacy fence. Nicole was crouched down, peeking through what must be a crack between the boards. Curious, Anna headed toward her.

Only one thing could engross Nicole so completely. Dusty Dare. Nicole was infatuated with her new uncle. Probably even more so, after the kitten episode this afternoon. Anna felt a lurch in her stomach as a thought occurred to her. What if Mr. Dare had a date, and they were, well, in his private pool making, er, doing private things?

Her heart began to thud as she made quick work of the incline. She didn't know why the image of her boss making love with a woman would affect her so negatively. His sex life wasn't her business.

She stepped onto the cement patio that surrounded the pool, trying to block out the sexy image her mind was forcing on her. "Nicole," she whispered, dreading that Mr. Dare would find out what his niece was up to, "what are you doing?"

The girl jerked around, then straightened, her eyes saucer-wide. Without a word she fled along the patio to vault a short flight of steps to the upper veranda and disappear into the house.

Anna propped her fists on her hips, frowning after the girl. There was nothing to do about it now, she supposed. Turning away with a tired sigh, she decided she'd speak to Nicole and never mention this to her boss. As she began to make her way back toward the lawn, she saw something sparkle where Nicole had been crouching. She looked down, worried that the teen had lost a necklace or an earring. Kneeling, she picked it up, only to discover it was just a shiny candy wrapper.

At that second, she glanced up. Between two boards that didn't quite meet, she could see a man emerge from the pool, broad shoulders gleaming with cascading water as he rose. His trim flat belly coming into view, he bounded up the pool steps, then—

The high-pitched gasp she heard startled her. It was another second before she realized the sound had come from her own lips and, worse, had been loud enough to be heard beyond the fence by a very gorgeous and very nude male, who was now wrapping a towel around his hips. Frozen, she could only watch as he looked accusingly toward the fence.

She knew what he was thinking and felt ill. With his angry expression burned in her mind, she managed to straighten, the urge to run—to save herself—strong within her. But that would be cowardly, and she would be acting no better than Nicole if she did.

"Who's out there?" he called.

Before she could manage to respond or figure out a way to shrivel up and disappear forever, the fence door slammed open and he was confronting her, dripping and angrier than she'd ever seen him.

"I might have expected something like this from Nicole," he said, his voice positively glacial. "Your boyfriend must be sadly lacking if you have to get your jollies ogling naked men."

She tried to breathe, but something wasn't working, and she was only able to take tiny hurtful pants. "I...I..." She gulped. "Mr. Dare, I know it must look—"

"The Andrews are quite a clan," he interrupted, taking a threatening step toward her. "A thief and a voyeur." With taunting deliberateness his fingers curved about the nape of her neck, and he tugged her into his damp embrace.

Demanding lips came down on hers, devouring their softness. Too stunned to react, she sagged against him, jolted by the intoxicating rage of his kiss. His hands locked against her spine, holding her to him with rough authority. His kiss challenged, mocked, yet somehow caressed, and her emotions bounced and skidded together in a cacophony of confused messages.

All too soon it was over, and he released her. As she staggered backward, slack-jawed, he warned softly, "Paybacks are hell, sugar. Next time, indulging in your kinky hobby will cost you more than a simple little kiss."

He strode away, and she stared after him, mortified by his scorn. At the same time, the unwanted thrill of his kiss, lingering on her mouth, made her giddy, unable to think clearly. Sinking to cement that still held the warmth of the day's sun, she slumped against the fence. Dusty Dare had caught her peeking at him—accident or not. He thought she'd been purposely spying—no, ogling him. Naked! Closing her eyes, she let out a humiliated moan.

But not all her despair was because of her embarrassment. She was mortified, too, by the fact that she'd never felt so alive in her life before tonight, never thrilled so completely to the touch of a man's lips!

Dusty Dare was all fireworks. She forced herself to recall her mother's warning. "Don't be fooled by fireworks, Anna. Fireworks fade. Marry a nice dependable man like Bruce." Thad was exactly the kind of man her mother would have loved. Nice and dependable.

With a shaking hand, she smoothed back a wisp of hair and tried to put thoughts of Dusty's sparklers-and-skyrocket kiss from her brain. But her brain wasn't buying. There was not going to be any forgetting that experience. A simple, little kiss, he'd called it. She exhaled long and low, rubbing her pounding temples. There was nothing simple or little about that kiss.

Still shaking, she managed to stand up and stumble off into the darkness. Suddenly it hit her. She had to meet with the man in—she jerked up her wrist to check her watch—in half an hour.

IN SOME KIND of cosmic cruelty, the minutes now flew by, and before she knew it, her watch said ten o'clock. Anna approached her boss's office with all the joy of a person who had a date with a branding iron. When she reached the door, she was sorry to see it wide open, so the instant she appeared in the doorway, she made a perfect target.

When she peeked in, he was absorbed in some papers and didn't appear to either see or hear her. She stood, hesitant, unwilling to begin this latest and possibly last confrontation between them.

"If you're waiting for me to take my clothes off, forget it," he said from behind a sheaf of papers. "You've had your freebie. Come in and sit down."

She jumped at the stringent sound of his voice. Without speaking and not sure she could if she tried, she crept into the office to take a seat in one of the antique chairs he no doubt kept there to make misbehaving employees as miserable as possible.

There was a long silence as he kept her waiting while he read—and read and read. She balled her fists, crossed and uncrossed her ankles. Counted the trophies in the trophy case, lost count in her nervousness, gave up and simply stared at the brown round-toed roper boots Dusty had propped on his desk. Her gaze moved of its own volition along rangy, indigo-swathed legs to a flat-bellied waist where a silver buckle glimmered. Continuing her unauthorized survey, she took in his rust-colored button-down shirt.

He was dressed in starched, tasteful cutter's basics, and he looked like a million bucks. Just as he had without clothes.

"Undressing me with your eyes, Miss Andrews?" he asked, sounding vaguely amused. "I feel so used."

Her gaze shot to his face. A malicious twinkle lit his eyes, and the corners of his mouth were tipped slightly upward. She blinked. "I was—" Stopping short in her heated defense, she recalled her vow not to talk back to him. She would appease this man at all costs. He could think what he wanted, say what he pleased. Nothing was as important as saving Steven from prison. Clamping her jaws shut, she sat still and met his bedeviling perusal straight on.

"So you admit it," he coaxed, putting the papers on the desk and placing his feet on the floor.

She swallowed. "Anything you say, sir," she managed in a tight whisper.

He cocked his head. A small frown wrinkled his brow. "What, no fiery denial, no hostile justification?"

Fidgeting, she recrossed her ankles, holding his dubious gaze with difficulty. "No, sir." Yearning for her inquisition to end, she decided to screw up her courage and get it over with. Her voice as raspy as the rustle of dry leaves, she leaned forward, pleading, "Please don't fire me, Mr. Dare. I'll do better. I won't argue or talk back. Just don't call the authorities about Steven. I'm begging you. And I know you won't believe this, but I really wasn't spying on you—it was an accident. I'll do whatever you ask, only give me another chance." Feeling as though she didn't have a scrap of air left in her body, she sank back into the chair, clutching its arms, fearful she'd sag all the way to the floor if she let go.

In the stillness, he watched her, his expression gradually becoming a stony mask, and Anna was at a loss as to what she'd done to make him angry this time. She'd tried her best to pacify him. All that was left was to leap over his desk and kiss his feet. What did the man want? Blood?

A momentary look of discomfort flitted across his face. He shifted in his leather chair, and it squeaked. He rested his forearms on his desk. "That was hard for you, wasn't it?" he observed quietly.

She nodded, not quite sure where this was going.

He steepled his fingers, his eyes boring into hers. "Miss Andrews, whatever other failings you might have, I have to admit you've got guts. That's more than I can say for your brother." Picking up his papers, he stood and walked over to stand above her. Holding out the papers, he added, "File these for me." Then without another word, he headed for the door.

Managing to grasp the pages before they dropped to the floor, she twisted around to stare at his back. "Is that it? Is that all you have to say? You only wanted me to file these? I . . . I begged you to let me keep my job for nothing?"

He turned, framed by the doors. "It wasn't for nothing, Miss Andrews. Let's say we both bared our . . . souls tonight." His lips lifted in a lazy smile. "I'd say your groveling makes us even."

"Well, I wouldn't." She jumped to her feet, her temper flaring. "You kissed me, remember!"

He inclined his head, inquiringly. "Do *you* want to kiss *me*?"

She felt a shiver of loathing—at least she chose to believe that was what it was. "I'd rather kiss muddy socks!"

It upset Anna to notice that her retort didn't douse the mocking twinkle in his eyes. He didn't even blink. Instead, he said, "Oh, one other thing. I'm having guests tomorrow evening. Twenty. We'll be taking a ride around the ranch at five. Have horses ready. Hunky will know which ones. And, of course, as my manager, you'll be expected to ride along.''

He was gone before she had a chance to respond, ask questions or throw a chair at his head—which is what she really felt like doing. He'd played a vindictive game, making her fret and wonder what he was going to do to her. Further payback, no doubt. Oh, how she hated the man!

There was a crackling sound, and Anna realized she was crumpling the papers he'd wanted filed. She stared down at them, feeling a mutinous urge to throw them into the air and walk out. Then it dawned on her. She was filing papers and going riding tomorrow night because as his *manager* she'd be expected to. She was still his employee, and he hadn't called the police about Steven.

Unsteady on her feet, she sank into the spindly chair and thanked Providence for giving her another chance, however agonizing the price.

CHAPTER FIVE

ANNA HAD BEEN AMAZED and relieved when the ride around the ranch with Dusty's guests went off without a hitch. Her boss had hardly spoken to her, which *hadn't* amazed her. Neither had the fact that, on the few times he had addressed her, his expression had been far from cordial.

As soon as she'd been able, Anna had slipped off to her cottage. Even though it was more than two hundred yards away from the pool, she could hear the hoots and laughter of Mr. Dare's boisterous guests as they ate barbecue and mingled, talking and laughing around the pool.

Anna had spent the rest of the evening trying to read a mystery novel but found the effort hopeless, her attention continually drawn back to the increasingly wild goings-on of Dusty and his friends. Finally she'd dropped off to sleep.

Over coffee the next morning she yawned, suffering from her lack of sleep, and wondered how Dusty was feeling. She squelched the thought. His unprincipled life-style was no concern of hers. Besides she had problems of her own, namely Thad, who had arrived bright and early both yesterday and today with new medication and an amorous glint in his eyes.

Shoving thoughts of both men from her mind, Anna headed for the practice pen to start training Freckle. Getting to work with Freckle was the one good thing that had come out of that ride around the ranch last night. Before she'd escaped, Dusty had pulled Anna aside and reluctantly admitted that the mare needed to be worked before some upcoming competitions. He'd made it clear he had no choice but to allow Anna to do it.

She smiled to herself. Freckle was a wonderful horse. Quick to learn. Her biggest weakness was some sloppiness in her turns, but Anna was sure she could cure the horse of that this morning.

She sat astride Freckle in the outdoor pen, watching a white-faced cow. Suddenly the cow tried to dash across the pen. Anna kept Freckle still for a count of two, then signaled her to turn. The mare dropped back on her hocks but not far enough to make the turn without touching her front feet to the ground. "Sweetheart, that's not good enough," Anna murmured, lightly touching the mare's flank with her spur to coax her to try harder.

The cow darted away from them, so Anna used leg pressure to get Freckle to break left, then right, then left again, keeping the horse's moves sychronized with the cow's. "Just keep your eyes on her, Freckle. Concentrate, sweetheart." The cow zigged right, and Freckle lurched that way. "Good eye, good eye," she whispered. Anna knew that training a horse was like raising a child. You had to make them respect you, but they responded better to love and a kind word than fear and abuse.

The heifer ran to the fence. The mare advanced, but Anna reined her in ten feet away. That way Freckle still had control over the cow, but wouldn't become pressed against the barrier or start depending on it to contain the cow. When the cow came off the fence, Freckle rolled back on her hocks a second time and made a smooth turn, blocking the heifer's escape. Elated by Freckle's swift improvement, Anna murmured, "Good girl. You didn't drop those front—"

"Punkin Pie," called a gruff old voice, "that mare'll be spinnin' on a shirt button 'for the day's out."

Anna grinned as her uncle limped out of the indoor arena to open the gate to the big round pen. As he stepped in, Freckle continued to control the cow in a series of textbook-perfect turns until the heifer stopped, giving up. Anna cued Freckle to stop working the little cow, then dismounted. Giving the horse an affectionate nuzzle, she looped the reins around the top rail.

"Uncle Bud!" She ran through the dust she and Freckle had stirred up to hug the old man. Due to his accident, he was a little stooped, making him just her height. "I didn't expect to see you here!" she cried happily, kissing his weathered cheek, which smelled of dust and inexpensive after-shave.

She stepped back to look at him. Bud Sawyer was a true old-time cowboy. From the top of his sweat-stained straw hat to his scarred boots and jangling spurs, he was a walking example of a proud and dying American breed. A breed of strong men, brave and uncomplaining, who ignored the danger and the damage inflicted on their bodies, because their work was as essential to them as breathing.

"What are you doing here?" she asked, her expression serious. "Anything wrong? You're feeling okay, aren't you?"

He chortled, his watery blue eyes filling with impish glee. Suspicion prickled along her spine. "What is it, Uncle Bud?" A thought hit her, and she grabbed his hands. "Is it Steven? Has he come back?"

Bud's smile faded and he shook his head. "No such luck, Punkin, but I think you'll be right pleased with what I've brought ya."

Anna was perplexed, but she followed him from the pen. Remembering Freckle, she yelled for Hunky, who had been repairing a fence nearby, to take care of the mare. Then she and Bud walked through the cavernous indoor arena until they were outside again and in front of the stable.

Parked on the gravel drive was a pickup and livestock trailer, which Anna recognized. They belonged to a neighbor of theirs, Euby Hobbs. He was helping Ben and Flint unload the trailer. When she caught sight of what they were unloading, Anna hoped she was having a nightmare. "Goats?" The word came out high-pitched and faint.

Uncle Bud chuckled and gave her such a healthy pat on the back she stumbled forward. "I know'd you'd be pleased, Punkin." He looked so proud, Anna's heart sank. How could she tell him to take them away? "Yeah," he was saying, "since Mr. Dare don't have no goats of his own, I figured the least we could do was loan him some of ours. Ain't he gonna be wild about having these bucks?"

Anna rubbed her hands nervously on the sides of her jeans. "He'll be wild, all right," she mumbled as she watched Euby, who was also her best client, help Ben and Flint herd the ten goats away from the truck.

"Well, Punkin," her uncle said, "where do you want 'em?"

"Uh . . ." Anna was at a loss. Goats were hard to contain, since they could climb or jump most fences. She could see Ben watching her, his chubby features tense with concern, as though wondering if he'd be judged guilty by association and fired once Mr. Dare found out about the goats. She wanted to reassure him that she'd take full blame, but she couldn't do it in front of her well-intentioned uncle. Bud had no way of knowing that her boss had prohibited her from using goats to train horses.

Stifling a weary sigh, she pointed to the south pasture. "Let's put them in there for now. With the trees along the back there'll be plenty of food to keep them happy for a while."

"Punkin Pie—" Bud took one of her hands into his warm, callused one "—me and Euby have to be getting back. He bought himself a couple of three-year-olds at a good price. They ain't been trained worth dirt, but I told him I can turn 'em around. Ol' Euby's countin' on me."

Anna gave her uncle another tight hug, her eyes tearing up. "Now don't you overdo things. You hear me? I'll be back to help as soon as I can."

"Heck, I'm gettin' along fine. Nobody to nag me 'bout what I can and can't stuff down my gullet." He winked. "How 'bout you?" he asked, his bushy gray brows dipping. "Ya look a mite weary."

Anna shook her head, managing to stifle a yawn. "Don't be silly. I'm fine. Even gave some vaccinations the other day."

Bud scrunched up his face. "Heckfire. Makes me sicker'n a calf with the slobbers just thinkin' about pokin' them animals."

Anna laughed at him. "Uncle Bud, that's always amazed me about you. You'll set your own broken bones, but you can't stand to watch anything or anybody get a simple shot."

He shook his head at himself. "Don't make no sense to me neither, Punkin. But I'd sooner be stuck up a tree with a mad ol' bear chawin' on my shorts than give shots. Glad I had old Doc teach you how to do it when you was a kid." He patted her cheek. "You'll do Mr. Dare proud. He's a lucky cuss to have you here till that darned fool brother of yours gets his backside outa trouble." The old man shook his head and moved toward the truck, mumbling something that sounded like, "If he lives that long." But, he'd spoken just as Euby had started the pickup's engine. So, she didn't quite catch it.

"What did you say?" she asked. "Was it something about Steven?"

He took off his hat and scratched his head, the curly crop of gray sparkling like new snow in the sunlight. "It weren't nothin', Punkin. You take care now."

"I will," she said, still confused about his remark. She must have heard wrong. "'Bye, Uncle Bud," she shouted over the roar of Euby's engine. "Now, don't you overdo!"

He waved his beat-up hat, then with a grimace, hauled himself into the truck. Anna bit the inside of her cheek. He was in pain, darn him. Why couldn't he admit he wasn't capable of physical labor anymore? Prideful old coot! He'd just climb on a horse, day after day, and get jounced around until he finally rattled his old bones to death. She watched, powerless to help, as Euby maneuvered the truck and trailer around and headed down the drive.

"What the heck are we going to do with them goats, Miss Anna?"

She turned to see Hunky, his work-toughened features full of worry, slap his hat against his leg, raising a cloud of dust. She'd learned that gesture meant he was really upset. He'd done it the whole first day she'd been on the job, and she'd hardly been able to see him because there'd been so much dust flying.

"Mr. Dare ain't gonna like having goats on the place," he muttered, wiping a grimy hand across his much-broken and very sunburned nose.

Anna shook her head. "You leave the goats to me, Hunky. Is Freckle cooled down?"

"No, ma'am. I was just gettin' to it when I saw them goats."

"You go back and take care of Freckle. I'll handle the—"

"Lambs! Little woolly lambs!" Nicole rushed out of the house, her garb a curious cross between Western and grunge. She wore ripped cutoffs and a black T-shirt, topped by an oversize, western-cut shirt. As she ran, her combat boots clomped loudly along the walk, and she had to clasp her new Stetson, a gift from Dusty, to her head to keep it from flying off. She bounded along the twisting path that weaved through Max's prized rose garden, at a perilous pace. "I've never seen lambs before. What are you going to do with them? Shave them and make sweaters or something?"

"Go ahead and take care of Freckle," Anna said to Hunky as Nicole skidded to a stop beside her. "They're not lambs, they're goats," she explained. "My uncle brought them for me to use to help train Mr. Dare's cutting horses." She decided not to add that Dusty was probably going to kill her the minute he saw the bearded little faces.

"Oh?" Nicole looked over to the field where the goats were. From a distance, they did look a lot like sheep— cream-and-gray creatures, the size of large dogs. They were hardly cuddly lambs, though. Each of the horned males weighed close to 150 pounds. But Nicole, being a city girl, wouldn't notice such subtleties. "Can I pet them?"

Anna was startled by Nicole's interest, since she'd refused to have anything to do with the horses and cattle. "Sure," she said, taking the girl by the hand. She walked with Nicole along the manicured lawn toward the fenced pasture where the goats were munching on the lower branches of the trees that lined the back fence. "They make great pets and will even come when you call them," she said. "They love poison ivy, too, which is wonderful, because there's lots on our ranch."

"Do they bite?" Nicole asked, obviously getting more nervous as they neared, for she could see now that they were fairly large.

"They can't bite. They've got teeth on the bottom, but only a hard gum on the top. Even if you stuck your fingers in their mouths it would only tickle."

"Cool," Nicole murmured, going through the white wooden gate.

Anna followed close behind. The grass in the pasture was knee-high, and wildflowers nodded in the warm humid breeze. It occurred to Anna that this would be the perfect time to speak to Nicole about why fifteen-year-old girls shouldn't ogle naked men. "That gray one with the twisted horn is Plague," she said, trying to think of a good way to broach the delicate subject.

Nicole scrunched up her nose. "Plague's a gross name."

"Uncle Bud and I named them after groups of things. A plague is a group of locusts." She pointed to a white-faced gray. "He's Murmuration, which is a flock of starlings." Indicating a cream-colored goat with gray spots on his back, she said, "And he's Troop, a group—"

"I know, I know," Nicole chimed in. "A group of Boy Scouts."

Anna shook her head and grinned. "Nope. It's a group of monkeys, but that was a good guess."

Nicole approached Troop, one of the smaller goats, and tentatively touched his back. "Troop's hair's nice. Sorta like a dog's."

"Like a German shepherd's, I'd say. Personally I prefer goats to other pets." A couple of the bucks lifted their heads and bleated, as though they agreed with Anna. "Speaking of pets, how's Scumbucket?"

Nicole laughed as Plague nudged her to get her to notice him. "Scumface is fine," she corrected, twisting so she could pet both goats. "Right now he's taking a nap in my tennis shoe." She squatted to stroke Troop's face, crooning to the animal as he rubbed his head against her hand. "

think I'm going to like living on a ranch, after all." Nicole glanced up at Anna with wide happy eyes. "I've never had pets before, and now I have a kitten and a bunch of goats."

Distress tightened Anna's stomach. How was she going to explain that their presence on Bent River Ranch was a mistake? How was she going to explain it to her boss? Her plan to talk to Nicole about the uncle-ogling problem slid away. She couldn't bear to chastise the girl now. Let her enjoy the goats while she could. There'd be time to talk about the other matter later.

"Hey, pardners!"

Both Nicole and Anna turned toward the shouted greeting. Thad was standing in the open stable door, waving his white cowboy hat.

"It's your geek friend."

"Thad's no geek," Anna chided. "He was a lot of help yesterday." Which wasn't a lie. He *had* been a help—considering he was a tenderfoot with a hay allergy. "I'd better go." She gave Plague one last pat. "I promised to teach Thad some riding basics this morning."

"Hey, Anna, before you leave, could you tell me all the goats' names?"

She smiled at the girl's interest. "Sure. That white guy's Exaltation, for a group of larks. Charm's over there. I think that's poison ivy he's eating, so leave him alone till he's done. Anyway, a charm is a group of finches, and—" she twisted around to point at an ivory giant with grand horns that swept back almost ten inches from his dangling ears "—that's Sloth, which is a group of bears."

When Anna was finished, Nicole said, "Weird names, but cool." She headed off toward Sloth with Plague and Troop tagging behind her.

Sloth looked up and bleated as Nicole straddled him and grasped his horns. "Giddap, Slothie!" Then Troop gave her a nudge and almost unseated her, which made Nicole laugh.

Since Nicole seemed content to play with the goats and Thad was calling her, Anna went to give the tenderfoot his riding lesson. She prayed her boss would take these latest additions to his household in relative stride—which, for him, would probably be a homicidal glare.

IT WAS FIVE O'CLOCK and the workday was finally ending. Anna had just left a pile of bills on Dusty's desk and was on her way back to he stable when Nicole crashed through the back door. "Anna! Anna! Uncle Dusty murdered Plague!"

Standing at the stove, a white apron around his waist, Max jerked around to gape.

"What do you mean?" Anna asked. She'd known her boss would be outraged about the goats, but she'd never dreamed he'd harm them. Oh, why did he have to come home early tonight? She'd hoped she'd have a chance to explain first. "You can't be serious, Nicole," she said, trying to remain calm.

Nicole shook her head, her loose black hair flying about her tearstained face. "No! No!" she bawled, her face screwing up in fresh agony. "Plague's lying out there—dead! Hurry!" She yanked on Anna's arm. "Hurry before he kills any more!"

Anna shot an apprehensive glance at Max, who was still frozen before the stove, his cooking fork aimed at the ceiling. "Would he?" she asked him as the hysterical girl dragged her toward the door.

The wizened old man's mouth had sagged open in shock, which to Anna was a good sign. Apparently Mr. Dare wasn't in the habit of massacring innocent creatures. She started to run toward the south pasture, but Nicole made an unexpected swerve to the right, yelling, "No. Over there—by the garage!"

Surprised, Anna changed course, vaulting the edge of the rose garden and dashing toward the four-car garage. Now she was beginning to understand what must have happened. Plague had leapt the wooden fence and gone off to investigate his new home. Why hadn't she foreseen this and staked him?

She was cursing her stupidity when she rounded the corner of the house and caught sight of Dusty Dare's black Mercedes. Plague was lying quite still on the car's hood.

Nicole began to shriek again. "Uncle Dusty, I loved him. I loved him!" She ran over to her uncle, who was examining the fallen goat. Nicole wedged herself between him and the car and began to pound his chest. "I loved you, too, but I can't love a goat murderer!"

Dusty was glowering, but to Anna he also seemed mystified. "Nicole, I don't think—"

"How could you?" she shrieked, cutting him off. He looked at Anna, seeming oblivious to the girl's pummeling. His all-too-familiar scowl told her he wanted an explanation.

She dashed to him, tugging Nicole away. "Nicole, stop that. Plague's not dead."

Nicole's sobbing didn't diminish, but she stopped fighting and wiped at her eyes with her fists.

"Plague's not dead," Anna repeated, then turned to Dusty. "What happened? What did you do?"

"What did I—" He halted in midsentence and glanced down at Nicole, running a hand roughly through his hair. He began again, his tone laced with annoyance. "I came home from work—which was obviously my first mistake—and went in to change my clothes. I was going to the stables to work Hazard when I heard clattering and discovered a goat on the roof of my car. I yelled and clapped my hands to frighten it off. It scrambled for a second, slid down the windshield and collapsed.''

"You frightened it, all right," Anna agreed, then she took Nicole's hand and led her to the car. "Nicole, Plague just fainted. Sometimes that happens when they're startled. It's rare, but not a bit fatal." Turning back to Dusty, she asked, "Would you mind lifting him down to the grass?" Her relief was so great that her goat wasn't dead that she was shaking—although she suspected that some of the shaking was caused by the scowl on her boss's face. She hadn't expected their goat discussion to begin quite this badly.

As he hefted the ungainly animal in his arms and placed it on the ground, Anna inspected the Mercedes. There were deep dents and scratches in the paint from Plague's hooves. Miserably, she turned to see Nicole kneel beside the goat. The girl squatted there, stroking its head and talking softly as it began to come to. With glistening eyes, she looked up and said, "Uncle Dusty?"

He shifted his gaze from the goat to her. "Yes?" he said, and Anna was surprised by the gentleness in his tone.

"I'm real sorry I hit you."

Dusty shrugged. "Don't worry about it. You were upset."

"I still love you, Uncle Dusty," she murmured. And it wasn't a lie. Anna could see the truth glimmering in her eyes.

Dusty cleared his throat, and Anna had the feeling he was blushing under that tan. But his discomfort didn't seem to last long, because he turned to her with a narrowed gaze and said, "Miss Andrews, I'd like to see you—*in private*." Then he headed toward the stable. Before she followed, Anna said to Nicole, "Please ask Hunky or Flint to stake Plague in the pasture. That'll keep him from straying."

The girl nodded and stood up as the goat struggled to its feet.

"Plague," Dusty muttered when she caught up to him. "Appropriate name."

"He's not named that because he's a bad goat," she protested. "A plague is the term for a particular group of things. You know, like a gaggle is a group of geese. A plague is a group of—"

"Goats?" he broke in sarcastically.

"Very cute." She was scared to death, but she refused to let him see it. "No, not a group of goats," she corrected, unsure what difference it made at this point. "A plague is a group of—"

"Andrewses?"

She gritted her teeth and counted to ten. They'd reached the stable, and Anna flung herself in front of him to stop him from going any farther. "Look, Mr. Dare, I'm sorry about the damage Plague did to your car. I'll pay for it."

He snorted derisively. "You're building up quite a tab, Miss Andrews." He started to say something else, then stopped and glanced away. His nostrils flared, and he seemed to be having some difficulty collecting himself. When he turn back, his expression was more resigned than angry. "Will you explain to me how I ended up with goat for a hood ornament?"

"I will if you let me."

He crossed his arms. "I'm listening."

"Okay." She dragged her upper lip between her teeth and took a deep breath. "They're here because it's my uncle's way of thanking you for not calling the police about Steven. He was so proud he could do this for you that I couldn't tell him to take them back. Don't you see?" She blinked away tears of frustration. "Uncle Bud thinks goats are a plus, not a—"

"Plague?" he supplied, but his tone wasn't harsh.

She swallowed, hard, and dropped her gaze to hide the tears that were threatening. "I . . . I was trying to figure out what to do with them. It's just that I didn't expect you back this early." Out of the corner of her eye, she could see Nicole leading Plague toward the pasture. He was such a sweet goat. He wouldn't hurt a flea—not on purpose, anyway. "You're so stubborn," she said bitterly. "If you'd just give them a try..."

"What, Miss Andrews? I didn't quite catch that."

She looked up at him, hoping her glistening eyes didn't give away her anguish. "I said, if you'd just give them a try, you'd change your mind."

"You're wrong, you know."

"I don't know any such thing!"

He must have seen Nicole's movement across the lawn, too, for he glanced in that direction and was silent for a minute. Gesturing toward his niece, he asked, "What's with her devotion to those damn things?"

Anna shrugged. "I don't know. It was like the kitten, I guess. Love at first sight. Goats are adorable animals, no matter what your opinion is." She paused, grimacing. "Nicole thinks they're hers."

He jerked back, eyeing her as though she'd shoved a gun into his ribs. "And you didn't tell her any different?"

She exhaled tiredly, recalling the happiness and gratitude in the girl's expression. "I guess I didn't want to upset her."

He laughed curtly. "Why is it, Miss Andrews, that you worry about everyone's feelings but mine?"

She was at a loss. "I . . . I've never wanted to upset you, Mr. Dare. I'm here to help." He raised an eyebrow, and the intensity she saw in his eyes made her shiver. Well, she'd pressed her luck pretty far and he hadn't lost his temper, so she decided to press further. All he could do was say no—which she knew was very likely.

"Mr. Dare, you came home early to work Hazard," she began, her voice breathy and unsteady. "Why don't we see who's right and who's wrong? Let me bring one of the goats to the round pen, and then you can work Hazard with him this evening. After that, whatever you decide, goes. Okay?"

He scowled at her—a scowl undoubtedly designed to make her wither up and drift away like ash in the wind. But she refused to allow that look to affect her. She stood as tall and straight as she could, hoping he couldn't see her legs shaking.

When he said nothing, she turned on her heel. "I'll go get one." Then she headed for the pasture, hoping that a boot to her backside wouldn't be her answer.

"This is a waste of time," he muttered behind her.

She made no reply and kept on walking. Holding her breath, she took a dozen more steps, before yielding to the temptation to look back.

He wasn't there.

She was stunned. He'd actually gone into the stable to saddle Hazard for a workout with one of her goats! Laughing in relief, she dashed off, a surge of joy filling her heart.

EASING BACK into the relaxed pose of a confident cutter, Dusty sat astride Hazard, the hand that held the reins poised above the stallion's neck and his heels pressed low in the stirrups.

There was no sign of tension in his broad shoulders as he had the stallion walk toward the middle of the pen. Anna and Hunky were on foot, shooing Plague toward horse and rider and preventing him from escaping either through or over the pipe fence.

Nicole and Thad sat on the top rail of the pen. Neither of them had ever seen a cutting horse in action, and both had expectant expressions on their faces. Thad grinned and winked at Anna, then sneezed so hard he almost fell over backward.

Anna returned the grin but quickly gave her attention to Dusty. His lips were drawn in a frown as he followed the goat's erratic movements. Of course, it could have been a frown of concentration, but Anna doubted it. Whatever his mood, he looked wonderful on that beautiful horse, and it was impossible to view him without a quickening of her pulse.

Somehow Anna tore her gaze from him, driving Plague toward Hazard as she murmured a silent plea that this would work. Plague ran in front of the stallion in his haste to dart through the fence. Immediately Dusty lowered his rein hand, giving Hazard the signal to go to work. The stallion dived low and headed Plague off with a sidestep that landed him between the goat and the fence.

Plague spun away, and Hazard anticipated his move. But the spunky little goat changed direction yet again, causing Anna to marvel at his speed and cunning. And she was thrilled by Hazard's reaction to this new challenge. Plague was fast and agile, but Hazard was a match for him, predicting his movements and blocking Plague's every attempt to get away.

Then the goat made an unexpected lunge to the left, and Hazard tried desperately to follow. Suddenly a masculine shout of alarm—or was it a curse?—split the air. When the dust cleared, Dusty Dare lay facedown in the dirt.

Anna gasped and rushed over to him. Hazard lurched right and left, thwarting Plague's escape for another second or two, before coming to a halt, allowing the goat to scramble under the lowest rail.

Hunky stood by the fence, stunned and speechless, as Anna dropped to her knees beside Dusty, who was raising himself up on one arm, spitting dirt. She mouthed a prayer of gratitude that he wasn't hurt. Nicole, she noticed, was chasing Plague.

Thad burst out laughing. "Boy, oh, boy, chief, you were bouncing around out there like a bad check!" His chortle seemed very loud in the otherwise quiet tableau. Anna shook her head in warning.

Dusty groaned, drawing her attention. He was sitting up and reaching for his hat.

"Are you okay?" she asked.

"Swell," he mumbled, slapping his hat against his outstretched leg.

Anna sat back on her heels and found herself fighting a smile. "I think that went pretty well, don't you?" She hoped the amusement in her voice escaped his notice.

He tugged his hat low on his dirt-streaked forehead and gave her an assessing look. "Did you know I was going to fall?"

She felt a blush warm her cheeks. "How could I know such a thing?"

Thad laughed again and Dusty glared at him. "Buckaroo Bob obviously isn't very fond of his teeth."

She couldn't hide her grin now. Unfortunately, Thad's laughter was contagious. "He doesn't mean any harm. He fell off Candy Cane twice today. I guess he figures that if a horseman as good as you can fall off, he's not so bad. And I think this is his way of bonding with you."

Dusty stood. "If that's the way he bonds, I'm surprised he's lived this long." Snatching up Hazard's reins, he started to limp away.

Anna jumped to her feet. "Do you want me to fetch another goat?"

He stopped, frowning. "Do I look like I want to eat more dirt?"

"Uh, no. Then, uh, what do you think about the goats?"

His lips twitched upward briefly, but then he was frowning again. "You don't want to know what I'm thinking about your precious goats."

When he began to move away again, she caught his arm. "Tell me." Her heart was soaring. She was positive she *did* know what he was thinking—that she was right. "Aren't they everything I said they were?" He was a fair man; surely even his wounded pride wouldn't let him it deny it. "Hazard was wonderful, too," she added, meaning every word. "I know why you love him so much. He's one in a million."

Dusty looked at her hand on his wrist, then her face. There was something odd, even gentle in his expression. "Finally we agree on something."

"And the goats?"

His gaze grew speculative. "Tell me one thing first."

"What's that?"

"Did you know I'd fall?"

She swallowed, her cheeks flaming. "Well, no, of...of course—"

"Now, now, Miss Andrews, your nose is growing." His ability to read people was plainly better than her ability to lie.

Embarrassed, she looked away, but she couldn't keep a tiny smile from her lips. "Well, maybe I, er, thought it might happen." She shrugged. "Most first-timers fall."

He chuckled, and she had a horrible feeling he believed she'd planned the whole thing. Which, of course, she hadn't. Not really...

She peeked at him. His eyes danced with devilment. "Miss Andrews, do you recall what I said about paybacks?"

She nodded, swallowing hard as a vivid memory of his hot kiss flashed through her mind. "They're... they're hell?" she recited timidly, dropping her hand from his arm. There was something entirely too intimate about the contact all of a sudden.

"Right." He reached up to touch his chin, where Anna noticed a small gash was beginning to bleed.

She flinched, not having realized he'd been cut. "And... and what about the goats?"

A smile played at the corners of his mouth. Then he tugged on Hazard's reins and ambled off, calling over his shoulder, "The goats, Miss Andrews, are hell, too."

CHAPTER SIX

AFTER ALL THE CHORES had been done, Anna escaped to her cabin, showered and changed, but not into her nightgown. Instead, she put on a pair of jeans and a cotton-knit top. For some reason, she was too restless to go to bed.

The night air was warm and inviting, and it seemed a million crickets were chirping soothingly in the distance. The bright moon beckoned, and Anna decided to go for a walk in the nearby thicket, hoping it would take her mind off...things. Besides, she rationalized, she hadn't really explored the thicket yet. Yesterday she'd noticed a winding footpath heading toward a creek. Just the sort of tranquil setting to calm frayed nerves.

She headed off at a brisk pace, trying to outrun the constant vision of a handsome man with "payback" glinting in his eyes. She stuffed her hands in her pockets. Darn his hide! Why did he have to be constantly in her thoughts? He didn't like her and she loathed him. He was attractive, yes. Charismatic, true. But he was too volatile. And too much like her father—a man she'd never known. A man who was never content. A man who always wanted something more, something new, something different.

Abe had left her mother when Anna was a baby. Her mother had said he was all fireworks, and whenever she'd talked about him there'd been both reverence and regret in her voice. Anna had grown to fear that kind of man—the kind who never really left a woman's heart, even after he'd left her life.

Dusty was like that. Daring, wonderful and dangerous. If a woman made the mistake of getting too close, she might not survive.

So why was she wasting time thinking about him? She shook her head. She supposed she was frustrated about Thad, and their on-again-off-again relationship. She knew he was trying, and she couldn't help being reminded of her stepfather once more. They were both solid steady men.

"You walk as loud as an elephant, sugar," came a deep familiar voice from somewhere in the darkness.

She twisted around, trying to spot him in the darkness. The path was shrouded in shadows, and she had no idea where he might be lurking. "Why...what..." she stammered. Sucking in a breath, she demanded shakily, "What are you doing? Practicing for a career as a mugger?"

"You've never heard of the ancient Indian art of stalking?"

She still couldn't see him. "I hate to break it to you, but stalking's a federal offense these days."

His low chuckle rippled through the night. Her reprimand was clearly of no concern to him. "I've brought good news," he said quietly.

"Good news?" she echoed, her heart leaping with the hope. "Steven's back!"

"Not that good, I'm afraid." He stepped into a shaft of moonlight, and she jumped at the movement, then stared. The silver radiance paid delicious homage to the muscular planes of his bare chest and shoulders. "Are...aren't you chilly?" she asked, her voice frail.

"It's muggy tonight."

She nervously shifted her gaze to his chin. There was no bandage. "How's the cut?"

He shrugged. "It was nothing. Do you want to hear the news?"

She nodded absently, unable to think about anything except his nearness. "I suppose so."

He stepped closer. Reflexively she stepped back, bumping into a tree.

"I'm going to let you work Freckle with the goats once a week."

"Really?"

He nodded but didn't smile. Still, she couldn't help reaching for his hands. "Oh, thank you, Mr. Dare. You won't regret it, I promise!"

He glanced at their joined hands, his surprise apparent, but no more so than hers when she realized what she'd done. Feeling foolish, she let go and self-consciously crossed her arms. "Uh, anyway, thank you."

He mirrored her actions, and she couldn't tell if he was doing it to mock her or if her touch had affected him, too. "Tell me, Miss Andrews," he asked abruptly, "how did your brother get into gambling?"

His change of subject caught her off guard, as did his show of interest. "I— Well, Steven once said he liked the excitement and the chance to get big money fast." She stuffed her hands back into her pockets and settled against the tree. "He's got a fairly big ego like—" She halted, bit her lip. She'd almost said "you." She blushed and turned away, though she knew he couldn't detect the blush in the darkness. "Anyway, it started small. You know, poker games with buddies. Then in the last year or so, he started playing for high stakes with some pretty tough guys."

"What do you mean, tough?"

"I don't know. He just seems scared. Once he even said something about getting his legs broken. But Steven's always exaggerated things."

There was silence, and she grew edgy waiting for him to respond, but she didn't want to look up. Maybe he'd left, not really interested in hearing about Steven. But now that Dusty had brought it up, fear began to niggle at her. "Mr. Dare, wait. You do think he's ex—" She raised her eyes then, and her question caught in her throat. She'd been wrong. He hadn't left. Instead, he'd come even closer. Mr. Ancient Indian Stalker had struck again.

She thought she saw worry in his eyes, but maybe not. It was quite dark. "You don't think anybody would really hurt him, do you?" she asked almost shyly. "I mean, I thought I heard Uncle Bud say something like, 'If he lives.'" She shook her head. "No. I must have heard him wrong. Don't you think?"

He looked contemplative for a second, frowning slightly, then after a few heart-pounding seconds, he placed his hands on either side of her and leaned forward, his lips perilously close to her own. "Sure. Don't worry."

He was so close, and he was staring at her with such interest that she lost her ability to speak. "I . . . well . . . I . . ." she stammered, dropping her gaze. Finally she managed to say, "Mr. Dare, you're making me nervous."

He chuckled. "I make a lot of people nervous. It keeps my competitors off guard and allows me to win. It's called good business."

What utter arrogance! She lifted her chin, refusing to back down. "Oh? I thought it was bad manners."

His laughter was deep and surprisingly warm. "By the way," he said, "your uncle called. Wanted to know how I liked the goats."

"Oh, Lord," she moaned, sagging against the rough bark.

"I told him Plague had me kissing dirt." His breath was gentle against her face, making her feel strangely dizzy.

"Bud thought that was very funny. He also had a lot of good things to say about his little Punkin Pie." He flashed a grin. "I was too sore to argue the point."

She was going to heatedly defend herself and her goat, but as she opened her mouth, his lips came down on hers. The intensity of his kiss was both thrilling and terrifying, and she couldn't bring herself to push him away.

With a sigh that held far less regret than it should have, she curled her arms about his neck and leaned into his inviting hardness. She relished the tautness of his muscles beneath her hands, knowing they were capable of great strength, though he held her in an embrace that was gentle, even tender.

His kiss was wild yet caring, demanding, yet giving. She clung to him, quivering, a current of raw desire spiraling through her. But just when she was about to abandon herself completely, he jerked away with a muffled curse.

She swayed backward, and the tree was the only thing that prevented her from falling. Staring into hard, frustration-darkened features, her voice breathy with yearning and sadness, she pleaded, "Why...why didn't you push me into some mud to pay me back? Why did you have to...to do that?"

"I wasn't—" He thrust a hand through his hair. "I didn't plan—" He cut himself off with another curse and stalked off. "Good night, Miss Andrews."

As he disappeared into the darkness, Anna lost her strength at last. Sagging to her knees, she wailed inwardly. *Please don't let me fall for Dusty Dare. Don't let me be that stupid!*

DUSTY STOMPED across the lawn to the pool, slammed open the privacy gate and dived into the chilly water. He was furious with himself for kissing Anna, and he needed cooling off. She might be irritatingly single-minded, and she might be the sister of a thief, and it was obvious she'd had a big laugh seeing him facedown in the dirt, but damn, he couldn't find anything wrong with her kisses. They were as soft as silk and hot enough to wither cactus. He was drawn to her like he'd been drawn to no other woman—back talk and goats and all!

Surfacing at the far end of the pool, he hauled himself out. "Blast it!" He yanked off a boot and heaved it against the privacy fence, the impact rattling the wooden slats.

What had come over him? He'd wanted to comfort and reassure her. Instead, he'd found himself kissing her! "You're an idiot, Dare," he muttered. "You're going to end up sending her brother to jail and then appropriating her home. You need to be making love to Anna Andrews like you need a goat for a hood ornament!"

THE MEMORY of Dusty's kiss nagged at Anna throughout the next morning. She felt guilty every time she saw Thad. Of course, she had been the kissee, not the kisser. But when she remembered how passionately she'd responded, she had to admit she'd done a little kissing of her own.

Thad sneezed, distracting her from her disturbing thoughts. He'd been cheerfully spreading sawdust in the stalls for the past hour, though his eyes were watering and his sneezing had become continuous. He put down his rake and went to the drinking fountain to splash his face and grab a few swallows. She wondered how he'd take the news that it was time for his riding lesson. It was noon, and she was hungry, but this would be her only break today. Thank goodness for Max—he'd noticed her lack of free time and had brought her a couple of sandwiches and a thermos of tea.

She saddled Candy Cane for Thad and Freckle for herself. Freckle deserved some fun after all her hard work, so Anna decided they'd go for a ride through the woods, which would be about an hour's trip with a novice rider in tow. "Okay, Thad," she called as she led the horses outside. "It's time to hit the trail."

A flash of distress crossed his features when he glanced at Candy Cane, but it was quickly gone. He grinned, though Anna had to admit it wasn't his best effort. "Well, little missy," he drawled in a truly feeble Western accent. "I'm as happy about that as a pie with flies on it."

She laughed at his mangled metaphor. "I think you mean you're as happy as a fly on a piece of pie—" she paused as a thought occured to her "—unless you're really not happy?"

He shrugged, wiping his brow with the back of his red-and-white checked sleeve. "I'm happy when you smile at me."

"What's wrong, Thad?" she asked, detecting the moroseness in his tone. "Don't you want to ride today?"

He eyed his mare distrustfully. "It's just...well, that horse hates me. It keeps throwing me. Don't you have one that's tamer?"

Anna shook her head. "The only way you're going to get a gentler horse is on a carousel." She stroked the little mare's cheek. "If you don't want to go, it's fine with me. I could use the time to do some paperwork." She held up the sack lunch. "We can just eat this in the stable, instead of the woods."

"The woods?" he asked, sounding much more enthusiastic.

"Don't get any ideas, Romeo. Mr. Dare's not paying me to fool around."

"That guy's not paying you at all."

"Yes, he is. Keeping Steven out of jail's the only pay I need." Indicating Candy Cane with a nod, she said, "Do we ride, partner, or not?"

He exhaled and rubbed his hands on his designer jeans, which were no longer pristine white. "Okay, Miss Kitty," he agreed with hollow enthusiasm. "We ride."

"Do you remember what I taught you, Thad?"

He approached Candy Cane slowly, as if the mare were a snarling beast with a taste for tenderfoot cowboys. "Yeah. I tell her 'whoa,' put my left foot in the stirrup, bounce on my right foot and just get up there."

"That's perfect," she agreed. "Now, you do that."

"What if she walks away and drags me the way she did yesterday?"

"She won't if you don't bounce up and down for five minutes," Anna said. "Go on." She swung up into her saddle. "It's easy."

"Yeah, just like swallowing a bus." Resigned, he grabbed the saddle horn and put his left boot into the stirrup, bouncing once, twice, three times. Candy Cane began to move forward, obviously trying to get rid of the irritation on her left side.

"Get up there, Thad," Anna instructed. On the sixth bounce, he finally lifted himself up, swung an ungainly leg over and landed heavily in the saddle.

"Super! If I didn't know better I'd have thought you were John Wayne." A small fib, but it put a grin on Thad's red face. "Okay. Now don't hold the reins so tightly—you're pulling her mouth." Anna lifted her rein hand. "Instead of using both hands, try it this way, with both reins in your right."

He did as he was told. "Think I like it better," he admitted. "I can grab the saddle horn easier if she tries to buck me off."

"Right." Anna resisted the urge to smile at the image of the gentle mare bucking like a bronco. "Now tap her with your heels and smooch her."

"I'm not kissing this thing!"

She couldn't hold back her laughter. "No, no. Make a smooching sound and she'll start walking."

He pursed his lips and smacked the air self-consciously, kicking Candy in the ribs with his heels. Obediently, the horse started forward.

"Good, now stick beside me and Freckle. Candy Cane'll do whatever Freckle does."

"Are you sure this nag knows that?" he asked, sounding more than a little nervous.

"Stay calm," she soothed. "You're doing fine." Anna walked her mare up beside Candy, and then together they moved toward the open field and the woods beyond. After a few minutes, Anna noticed that Thad still looked ill at ease, and her heart went out to him. "How're you doing?" she asked.

"Great," he said from between clenched teeth, then he sneezed. "Just great," he muttered, and tugged a handkerchief from his hip pocket to dab at his nose.

There was a thudding sound to Anna's left. She turned in time to see Troop bolting across the yard with Nicole in hot pursuit. Anna reined Freckle but had no time to tell Thad what to do. The goat swerved right into Candy Cane's path, and the horse reared, causing Thad to lose his balance. He grabbed wildly for the saddle horn, but missed and toppled to the grass.

As Candy galloped back to the stable, Anna jumped down from Freckle and hurried to Thad's side. "Are you hurt?"

He lay sprawled on his back, his hat pushed over his face. "Just leave me here and let me die."

Anna lifted the wide brim, and he squinted as the sun hit in his eyes. "Would John Wayne have talked that way?"

He struggled to sit up. "No," he said despondently. "He probably would have said, 'Just leave me here to die, pilgrim.'"

Anna patted his arm affectionately. "If you can joke, you can ride."

"Oh, yeah? I've never seen Joan Rivers on a horse." He plucked his hat from her hand and tugged it down so low on his head his ears splayed out. "I'm sorry, sweetie, I—" he sneezed violently "—don't think I'm cut out for riding those things." He swiped at his nose with his handkerchief, muffling his words. "The only way I ever get off is by being thrown on my butt."

She smiled sympathetically and gave him a hand to help him up. "It could have happened to anyone, Thad. Don't be upset. You've still got three days of vacation left."

"Gee, thanks, rub salt in my wounds," he groused, jamming the handkerchief back into his pocket.

Laughing, she looked around and spotted Nicole, still chasing Troop. They were heading toward her and Thad again. "Why don't you take our lunch to my office." She handed Thad the bag. "I'll be there in a minute."

He nodded, dusting off his backside with a painful grimace. "I might as well sell my chairs. I'll never sit down again."

She stifled another giggle. It wasn't nice to laugh at a someone in pain. "Sorry, Thad." By way of apology, she kissed his cheek. "I'll help Nicole with Troop and be right with you."

Her kiss seemed to cheer him immeasurably. "See you, sweetie."

She ran over to head off Troop. After a couple of minutes of darting and blocking, she and Nicole got the goat to stop running. "He gnawed through his rope," Nicole explained, wheezing from exertion. "And he—" she swallowed "—got in Max's flower garden and ate some stuff."

Anna felt dread sweep through her. "Stuff?"

The girl nodded, nervously chaffing her hands. "Like roses and, uh, stuff..."

"Oh, no!" Anna moaned. "Not Max's prize roses?"

Nicole screwed up her face. "I don't know. Which were the prize ones?"

"All of them."

Anna turned reluctantly and saw Dusty standing a few feet away in a black suit and red power tie. "I'd say the goat ate about four thousand dollars' worth, give or take."

Troop burped.

"I'll give your compliments to the chef," Dusty added sarcastically.

Anna's mouth went dry. "Does Max know?"

"I'd say so. He's looking up recipes for goat chili."

Anna heard Nicole's gasp and glanced at her. "He's kidding," she assured the girl, hoping she was right. "Take Troop to one of the stalls we kept the goats in last night."

Nicole looked worried. "Were you kidding, Uncle Dusty?" she asked cautiously.

"Max won't hurt the goat, Nicole," he said softly, but Anna thought there was a hint of irritation in his voice.

Nicole smiled, apparently satisfied. "Tell him Troop didn't know he was being bad, Uncle Dusty. I'll give him a good talking to." Her eyes sparkled with affection and gratitude. "Are you gonna be here for lunch?"

He nodded. "I don't have another meeting until four, so I thought I'd eat and then work Hazard." He turned to Anna. "Have Hunky get him ready."

As Anna nodded, Nicole shouted, "See you in the house, Uncle Dusty." He acknowledged her with a wave as she tugged the goat toward the stable by the stubby piece of chewed hemp. "You don't eat rope or roses, dummy," she scolded.

Anna faced Dusty. She focused on his chin, for looking directly into his eyes bothered her. Noticing the bruise and cut on his jaw, she asked, "How's the face?"

He seemed confused, charmingly so. She would have enlightened him, but decided it was foolish to remind him of one other goat catastrophe in a rapidly growing list and changed the subject. "It was sweet of you not to shout at Nicole."

He didn't answer immediately, and in the tense stillness Anna could hear a couple of blue jays squawking nearby. They sounded annoyed. She knew her boss was, by the flexing of his bruised jaw, and she wondered if he was about to squawk at her. "They aren't Nicole's goats, Miss Andrews. Why should I shout at her?"

Dusty was no longer smiling, and her stomach lurched. "I'm terribly sorry, I'll—"

"I know," he interrupted, a dispirited note in his voice. "You'll pay for it. I've heard that before."

She stood mutely, suddenly aware that the breeze had changed directions, for she could now smell Dusty's cologne. Her pulse quickened in response. Disliking her reaction, she became impatient to leave. "Well, I'll get back to—"

"You'd better reinforce the pasture fence with wire mesh to keep them in," he said unexpectedly.

"Of course, that would help, but the expense—"

"Would be considerably less than what they've cost me so far."

Needing to get away, she took a step backward. "I—I'll go apologize to Max after I take care of Freckle and talk to Hunky."

"Order that wire mesh today so it'll be here in the morning."

"Yes, sir," she murmured, taking a second and third step away from him. "I'll get on that after—"

"I noticed the boyfriend's riding expertise," he commented, veering off the subject. "You might suggest he fall off farther from the barn, to help cure Candy Cane of being barn sour."

Anna had carefully avoided his eyes, but at his gibe, her gaze shot to his. "He was doing fine until Candy Cane shied." She took a deep breath to control her temper, but that was a mistake, because it just forced her to inhale more of his scent.

"What do you see in that guy?" he asked. It could have been a casual question, but it wasn't—his voice was ever so slightly strained.

Not sure what to say, she lowered her glance to his polished shoes. They gleamed in the sunlight, irksomely flawless and unscuffed. She knew exactly how she looked—grimy with dust and sweat. She smelled of horses, too. With monumental effort, she straightened her shoulders and stared directly into his disquieting eyes. "Thad's a good man, Mr. Dare. Hardworking. Steadfast. Trustworthy. We've had our differences, but he loves me and . . ."

"And you love him," he finished for her.

She was unable to read his closed expression, and that made her restless, so she grabbed Freckle's reins. How was she to answer? She cared deeply for Thad. That much was true. No other man had ever tried so hard to please her. Besides, hadn't her mother always cautioned her not to be fooled by glitter and flash?

Her mother hadn't been in love with her stepfather when they'd married, but she'd respected him. Love had grown between them over the years. Anna knew her affection for

Thad would grow into love—with time—just as her mother's affection for Bruce had. But she couldn't exactly tell Dusty Dare that. In a tight whisper she replied, "My feelings are none of your business. However, if you must know, I love Thad very much." It was only a tiny lie. Practically the truth, in fact.

The rancher studied her for a long moment, as though trying to read her thoughts. She held her brave pose, struggling to control the twisting knot in her stomach. Those eyes of his were simply too discerning.

"I see," he said at last, his smile little more than a baring of teeth. "Then, good luck to you and your Bronco Billy."

"Why should you care how I feel about Bronco, er, Thad?" she blurted, wondering why she was asking the question.

"I don't give a damn, Miss Andrews. I just think there's more to forging a relationship than buying Western clothing and falling off a horse a few times."

"Oh, you do?" she returned. "I'm dying to hear your opinions, Mr. Dare, since you're so great at relationships!"

He scowled down at her. "What does that mean?"

She didn't know exactly. She had no idea why she'd said it. Where had her mind been? Obviously not connected to her mouth. "I, uh... Well, you're not married or anything."

His dark eyes glittered angrily, but she managed not to cringe. "Maybe I'm not married because I don't play games. Maybe I'm not married because I don't intend to be like my brother. Maybe I want to find a woman who can share my life and my passions. Is that all right with you?"

His features were rigid and uncompromising. She felt an unwelcome thrill at the conviction she heard in his words. But she tamped the emotion down and said, "I couldn't care

less!'' Then she spun away to grab Freckle's dangling reins
and head for the stable. Some cruel inner voice fairly
shouted, *Just think what it would be like to be loved by that
man.* She forced the voice to be silent. *It would be horrible!*
she told herself. No matter what Dusty Dare said, he'd never
be satisfied to share his life with only one woman. He would
tire of her and leave—just like her father.

Anna supposed the worst flaw a fireworks man could
possess was the inability to realize how fickle he really was.
Her father had vowed eternity to her mother, once. But his
version of eternity had been very short indeed.

DUSTY WAS AWAY on business quite often during the next ten
days, which was fine with Anna. But out of sight did not,
unfortunately, put him out of mind. She thought constantly about his kisses, his scent, the feel of his warm skin
under her hands.

Thad's vacation had ended, and he'd gone back to managing Tulsa's Elite Hotel, so Anna saw little of him. But they
still had a couple of late dinner dates and a few ''I love you''
calls before she went to sleep.

Even when he was around the ranch, Dusty made no attempt to see her. Several times, while she ate dinner, Max
had come into the kitchen with her instructions for the next
day, minutes after she'd heard Dusty's footfalls. Invariably
she'd lost her appetite, knowing he was close, yet entirely
disinterested in speaking to her.

This morning's message had been a written one. It read,
''We leave for Tahlequah at five tonight. Have Freckle in the
trailer with two turnbacks and two herd holders.'' He'd
added a most unsettling postscript. ''You'll ride her in the
three-year-old class. Consider it a test.''

She'd known about the competition, but hadn't expected
to go. She glanced uneasily at her watch. It was four-forty-

five, and she'd been pacing beside the truck for ten minutes. Deciding that was a waste of energy, she climbed into
the cab to stare absently out the windshield. A hawk rode a
warm updraft, slowly, easily, silently. Watching such beauty
usually eased her spirits, but today, every time the hawk
spiraled upward, it only reminded her that another minute
was gone, and soon she'd have to face Dusty Dare.

Freckle and the four other horses they'd be using during
tomorrow's competition were in the shiny thirty-foot trailer.
Dusty certainly spared no expense when it came to his
horses. It was a top-of-the-line model, as was the black and
silver pickup it was hitched to.

Anna slumped back in her seat, closing her eyes and trying not to fidget. But her restless fingers played with her
long braid as she prayed to do well. She hadn't been in many
competitions, but she'd trained a lot of working cutters. All
she needed to do was relax and convince herself that she was
simply cutting cattle.

To make matters worse, she had no news about Steven.
She'd hoped that, after nearly three weeks, he would have
come to his senses and returned the carving.

She twisted and retwisted her braid, fearing that this ride
to Tahlequah would be about as pleasant as straddling a
barbed-wire fence. But she vowed she wouldn't crumble, no
matter how nasty Dusty was. The most important thing was
for him to see how well Freckle was responding to her
training.

She'd grown to love that mare over the past few weeks.
Freckle was the finest horse she'd ever trained. And if
Freckle won tomorrow, it would go a long way toward
proving that Anna was worthy of training Hazard, too.
Rubbing damp palms on her jeans, she tried to be calm, but
so much depended on the competition. Sometimes she

wasn't sure she'd be able to stand upright, let alone stick in the saddle and win.

Her reverie was broken when Dusty opened the door and got into the driver's seat. Clad in body-molding jeans, an Oxford shirt, black boots and a black Stetson, he was the epitome of a sexy cowboy. When he'd settled himself, it struck her that his shoulders took up an awful lot of room. Reflexively she slid closer to the door. He seemed to notice her withdrawal and gave her a long look. But he made no comment before turning to start the engine.

Apparently he'd decided to give her the silent treatment. She jutted her chin stubbornly. *Okay, Mr. Dare,* she declared inwardly. *You're not the only one in this truck who can play that game!*

CHAPTER SEVEN

CLENCHING HER HANDS into fists, Anna stared out the window as they drove along the highway. Though the road was paved, Anna had the sinking feeling that the hour-and-a-half trip to Tahlequah was going to be one rough ride.

After a few minutes, she glanced surreptitiously at his profile. There was no doubt he was attractive, but there was a hard uncompromising quality about him that disturbed Anna. What if she didn't win tomorrow? Wishing she was going to face something more pleasant—like have a tooth drilled—she turned to gaze out the window at the undulating green countryside, but saw none of it. She was too busy trying to relax.

"How are things going?"

After fifteen minutes of dead quiet, his question startled Anna so badly she nearly shrieked. Managing to mask most of her surprise, she asked evenly, "With my brother or the ranch or Freckle?"

A halfhearted smile lifted the corners of his mouth. "Don't panic. I was just making conversation. I can see things at the stable are under control."

She was confused by his unexpectedly civil attitude. She looked at him, her gaze sweeping along his lean cheek to the chiseled lines of his jaw to check for a jumping muscle. There it was. He was provoked about something, but he was trying to hide it. She wondered what it was. "Well, if you mean Steven, I'm afraid nobody's heard anything from him. Not even his friends. It's as though he's been swallowed up by the earth." She kept her eyes trained on him, no matter how difficult it was to watch his jaw jump and bunch.

He looked at her briefly, but said nothing. Silence again stretched between them and became so disturbing she felt compelled to say something. "Don't worry, Mr. Dare. I know he'll do the right thing in the end. Steven's made some mistakes, but he's really a good—"

"You don't have to keep making excuses for your brother, Miss Andrews. No matter what happens, you've done your best."

Caught off guard by his generosity, she didn't know what to say. "That . . . that's kind of you," she managed finally. Dropping her gaze to her fists, she prayed that the Ross Sixkiller carving hadn't been damaged. For the first time she truly believed that the man beside her didn't want to put her brother in jail or take away their ranch. Still, if Steven had allowed that carving to be damaged, Dusty would be justifiably angry, and he would probably have no choice but to take punitive action. From what Max had told her about him, Dusty's Cherokee heritage meant more to him than just about anything.

"How's the boyfriend?"

She glanced at him, not sure she'd heard him right. "How's what?"

"Mr. Hotel," he said.

She heard the disdain in his voice, and it irritated her. "I don't understand why you don't like Thad. He spent a week at your ranch, freely giving his time to help you out."

He arched a brow skeptically. "To help you out of your clothes, you mean."

She gasped. "That's vulgar and rude and—"

"And true," he interrupted coolly. "But you'll say it's none of my business."

"That much is true, anyway!" She shot him a quelling look, resentment at his audacity sweeping through her. "If you want to talk about business, Mr. Dare, that's fine, but leave my personal life alone."

She watched him clench and unclench the wheel as though he were trying to ease tense fingers. "I've lost my urge to chat," he said.

"Maybe that's just as well. We don't seem to be able to talk without fighting, anyway."

He was scowling, but as she watched, his lips began to twitch. "We kiss rather well, though, don't we?" She gasped. "Cat got your tongue, sugar?" he taunted.

"I'm not discussing my tongue with you," she retorted, oddly breathless.

His chuckle was low and unsettling as he returned his attention to the highway.

The man was incorrigible. But that was the hallmark of a fireworks man, she supposed. She exhaled loudly, thinking very unladylike thoughts.

Smiling at the sound, he exited from the main highway, and Anna realized they were nearing Tahlequah. Twenty minutes later, he said, "Once we get the horses into their stalls, I thought we'd eat at Lou's Diner. It belongs to a cousin of mine."

She was startled by the invitation. "I . . . I think I'll skip dinner. I don't feel much like food."

They rode on for several miles before he asked, "Are you sick?"

She shook her head, not wanting him to know how nervous she was. "Sometimes I don't eat dinner," she fibbed.

He pulled into the arena's blacktop parking lot and stopped the truck near a long red barn. "You look pale," he said after a few moments. "Are you pregnant? If you are, you shouldn't be riding in a competition like this."

She blinked. He was certainly full of surprises today. But he was all wrong this time. "Of course I'm not pregnant."

"Then why do you look so sick? And why won't you eat dinner with me?" A flash of frustration lit his eyes. "Do you hate me that much?"

"I don't hate you!" she assured him, amazed by the degree of conviction in her voice. "If you must know, I'm terribly nervous. I want Freckle to win very badly so you can see..." She faltered, wishing she'd never opened her mouth.

He looked as if her admission surprised him. He turned away and pulled the key from the ignition, then turned back, worry marring his features. "Look, Miss Andrews, I know I've taken a lot of my anger at your brother out on you, and I apologize. You've done a pretty fair job as my manager. And believe it or not—" he grinned "—my horses don't win every competition they're entered in. But don't let that get around."

She was so amazed by his kindness she had no idea how to react. When she didn't speak, he continued more seriously, "Don't kick yourself around the barn if Freckle doesn't take first money tomorrow. Do your best. Have you ever competed here before?"

She shook her head. "Hardly anywhere. Mainly I train horses for cattle ranches, not competitions."

He pursed his lips, nodding. "Right. You told me that. Okay. Just remember—the ground's harder here than at Bent River, so Freckle won't stop as hard because there'll be more shock to her feet. Don't let it fluster you."

He put his arm along the back of the seat as he spoke. She could feel the heat of his flesh near her shoulder. "You won't have to urge her to run," he was saying, "because she's already on faster dirt. The hard ground might make

her want to be more chargey than usual, so be ready to give
her some cow-side leg pressure to move her away." He
smiled again, encouragingly, and the sight of it made her
heart beat faster. "Just do what you always do and forget
about everything else. You'll be fine."

She sat there speechless as he moved to open his door.
"Max reserved rooms for us at the hotel across the street.
You take care of registering Freckle and I'll stable the
horses." He paused, and she waited, wondering what he was
thinking. "By the way, Miss Andrews, there's a powwow in
the park tonight," he said. "After you check on the horses,
you might want to relax and watch the dancing. I have relatives in town, and we're all going, so if you'd like to join
us, I'll come by your room to get you."

She was curiously surprised and disoriented. He'd never
treated her like an equal before. and his expression seemed
almost caring. Maybe, for the briefest moment, he'd recalled how it was to be nervous. She managed a weak smile
of gratitude, but she didn't want his pity. "Thanks, but I
think I'll stay in. I'll just give Thad a call and hit the hay
early."

A hint of displeasure crossed his features, but it was
quickly gone. Then he nodded once and left her.

"HELLO, THAD," Anna said with a smile when he answered the phone. She'd taken off her boots and was
lounging on a "barren wilderness"-patterned bedspread.
Her motel room was done in uninspired Western decor. But
it was clean and cool. The phone worked, the sink didn't
drip, and it was close to the arena. What more could she
ask?

"Hi, sweetie," he replied. "I called the ranch, and they
told me you were going to Tahlequah for a competition."

"Yes, that's where I'm calling from," she told him, nervous again at the reminder of tomorrow. "Wish me luck?"

"Sure. Good luck," he said, then paused as though he wanted to say something more. "So," he finally asked, "why are you there tonight if the contest isn't until tomorrow?"

She detected a note of jealousy in his tone but chose to ignore it. "Mr. Dare has family here. He's visiting them tonight."

"Oh, okay." Thad sounded appeased, then hurriedly changed the subject. "Sweetie, the reason I was trying to call you is that I have news."

"News? Is it Steven?"

"Yes. One of his buddies got in touch with me when he couldn't reach you or your uncle Bud."

"But Uncle Bud should be home."

"Oh, he was probably out at the barn. You know he can't hear worth squat. Anyway, this buddy said Steve had spent some time hiding out with an old girlfriend in Dallas. Unfortunately he's not there anymore, but the guy said the girlfriend told Steve about Dare's deal. That was a couple of days ago. So, I figure it's just a matter of him getting up the nerve. He could be on his way home. At least, that's what his friend thought."

Anna's vision blurred with tears of relief. "Oh, Thad, that's terrific. I'll tell Mr. Dare right away." She slammed down the receiver and reached for her boots. When she'd gotten the first one halfway on, she realized she'd hung up on Thad. For a minute she toyed with the idea of calling him back, but decided she could do it later. She wanted to tell Dusty the news immediately.

The park where the powwow was taking place was easy to find. She simply followed the stream of people, many of whom were clad in feathers and beads. She passed the cut ting arena and went through a stand of trees into a field at the far end of the park.

She'd never been to a powwow before, though she'd seen them mentioned in the Tulsa paper. Not being Native American, she'd always assumed the participants would frown on strangers. That didn't seem to be the case, however.

The atmosphere was open and welcoming, just like a carnival. The mown field was dotted with brightly colored tents where people hawked chili dogs, hamburgers, tacos and native crafts. Most everyone was dressed exactly as Anna was—jeans, T-shirts and boots—but a distinctive few were clad in tribal costumes. Even in her excitement about her brother, she found herself fascinated by the colorful regalia.

The most unusual feature of the powwow was a large crescent-shaped structure, which seemed to be used solely for shade. It was constructed of cut trees that were stripped of their limbs and placed in a wide half circle. Leafed branches had been lashed together to form a covering. The whole structure appeared to be about fifty feet long and ten feet wide, and beneath its canopy of branches, closely packed spectators sat on folding chairs or blankets just outside a makeshift grassy arena.

It was eight-thirty, so there was about half an hour of daylight left. She could hear a drumbeat begin in the distance. She looked toward the sound and saw a canopied drum in the center of the adjacent arena. Encircling the huge instrument was a group of men, all beating it and chanting in unison.

This was soon accompanied by a chorus of chants as another group of men, women and children, dressed in vivid traditional clothing of leather and beads, began to dance around the drum. Intrigued, Anna walked toward the performers.

The grassy dancing arena was separated from the spectators by a circle of long wooden benches. Apparently these were for the use of the dancers, because the few people who were sitting there were dressed in feathers, beads and hides, their faces painted with bright colors and what looked to Anna like ancient symbols.

On the unshaded side of the arena, behind the benches more spectators lounged on blankets in the grass, eating food purchased from booths and enjoying the dancing. A few children were asleep, oblivious to everything. Anna noticed that most of those in the crowd were Native Americans, but others seemed merely interested spectators like herself.

She glanced around, looking for Dusty. Behind her was a large, red-and-white-striped tent, its flaps opened both in front and back for ventilation. Inside, tables were spread with crafts for sale. She decided that was as good a place as any to start her search for Dusty.

She didn't see him when she entered. Considering his height, he would have been hard to miss. She was about to leave, but decided it would be a shame to go without looking at the tables. There were hand-tooled leather belts, earrings made of beads and feathers and beautiful silver jewelry.

A table full of bright shawls caught her eye. She fingered one of the woollen ones. It was red decorated with a design in shades of green and gray that she was sure must have some significance. But the white-haired octogenarian behind the table was busy with another customer, so Anna left the tent.

As she searched the crowd for Dusty, a man with long gray braids began speaking over a public-address system a the far end of the arena. "Before we get back to the men's dance competitions, I'd like to say it is our hope that you all enjoy your visit with us." His smile was broad. "And for our non-Indian friends who have joined us today, may you leave with a better awareness of and respect for our culture." He held up both hands in a gesture that embraced the audience, the fringe of his beaded shirt ruffling in the breeze.

With his arms held out that way, he reminded Anna of the bronze statue of the Indian brave that had stood in the hallway of her high school. She'd never thought much about the significance of that statue back then, but now, watching this elderly man, she was ashamed of her ignorance and her indifference.

As the elder spoke, his voice rang rhythmically, reminding her of the drum she'd heard earlier. "Some of you, new to our intertribal powwows, may not know this, but we use these celebrations to commemorate the many Native Americans who have fought and died for this country in its wars."

Anna heard the emotion in his voice and felt it in her own heart.

"Now, one of our favorite competitions is about to start," he added, his tone brighter. "The Fancy War Dance. So, those of you entered in the competition, please take your places around the drum."

Fancy War Dance? Anna looked for her boss once again, but without success. Maybe he'd been delayed with his relatives. With a shrug, she decided to watch the men dance, and she took a seat on the grass beside a young woman holding a sleeping newborn.

The woman smiled at her. "Hi. I'm Sue Wahweotten—Creek-Cherokee-Delaware. And you?"

Anna was confused at first, then realized that, with her long braid, she probably looked at least partly like an Indian. She smiled back. "Anna Andrews. French-Danish-English. I'm just here looking for someone."

"Oh," Sue said. "Your first powwow?"

Anna nodded. "What's this they're getting ready to do?"

Sue glanced toward the grassy field, where men were gathering, their costumes more ornate than most Anna had seen.

"This is the fancy dance competition. It's developed from ancient war dances and depicts victory and bravery. It can get pretty exciting when the drums start beating really fast, and the guys are doing intricate steps with lots of twirling and jumping. It's my favorite to watch. Real sexy." She grinned sheepishly. "My husband was in the grass dance earlier. His costume's made with long yarn all over it to simulate tall prairie grasses. That dance is great, but tame compared to this dance." She laughed, her cheeks pinkening. "These guys have to be in really good shape to dance the way they do. It takes stamina and a lot of muscle to win. Mind you, an old married lady like me isn't supposed to notice."

Anna looked back out over the assembled men. They were wearing brightly beaded moccasins of every imaginable color with some sort of fur at the ankles.

Sue pointed to a nearby dancer's head. "See that crown he's wearing with the two feathers sticking out?"

Anna nodded.

"That's called a roach. It's made of porcupine quills and stiffened fur. And the big fan of feathers jutting back from their shoulders and waist are bustles, made from eagle feathers." She must have seen Anna's wince at the idea of someone taking the feathers from an endangered species because she added quickly, "Don't worry. Eagles aren't hurt to get them. Those feathers have been shed by the birds and are gathered from nesting sites under strict supervision. And if there's a shortage of eagle feathers, they use dyed ones from turkeys."

As her companion spoke, Anna heard jangling. She saw now that most of the men wore bells on leather strips tied below their knees.

One man entered the arena just then and captured her attention. His back was toward her, but she could see he had a powerful upper torso. He wore a beaded leather vest that was stitched in geometric patterns of red on black with flashes of silver. His fringed loincloth echoed the pattern and colors, revealing well-muscled legs. Forcing her gaze away from his legs, she noticed a wide beaded band girdling his upper arm from which a smaller circle of feathers jutted—similar to the two at his back. She could just see one tanned forearm, which was sheathed from his wrist midway to his elbow with a black-and-red beaded cuff.

The warrior stopped to talk to another contestant. He was now turned toward her, and Anna saw that his face was half covered in red paint, from the middle of his forehead, where it met a black-and-silver headband to the tip of his straight nose. Two black strips ran from the outer corner of his eyes to his dark hair, and there was another across the bridge of his nose.

She squinted at the man, a sense of awareness nagging at her. At that instant a heavy drumbeat filled the air, and the contestants began to bob and chant in time. As the man she'd been watching moved, revelation struck her. It was Dusty! She must have gasped, because Sue took her arm and asked, "Are you okay?"

Unable to tear her eyes from the man doing the hauntingly graceful war dance on the grassy field, she whispered, "That's Dusty Dare!"

"Oh, yes, he's a past champion, but he doesn't make it back here very often, especially since his father died. Isn't he wonderful?"

Watching Dusty and the other contestants was definitely a breathtaking experience. Strong, male bodies whirled about the field, imparting the spiritual eloquence of a little-known ancient American culture. The drumbeat quickened, and the chanting became louder, punctuated by an occasional whoop from the dancers. Now the men were twirling and spinning like dervishes to the fevered drumbeat, and Anna was riveted.

As she sat there, entranced, the sunset cloaked the sky in bloodred glory.

CHAPTER EIGHT

"WHY MUST THERE BE fireworks in everything you do?" she murmured sadly, drawing Sue's curious gaze away from the dancers.

Realizing the woman next to her was peering at her inquiringly, Anna forced a grin. "The war dance is pretty spectacular—like fireworks," she said, hoping she'd fooled Sue.

The drums halted, and so did the contestants. They held their poses, and several jeans-clad judges walked among them, asking some dancers to leave. Dusty and nine others remained after half the men sat down.

"What happens now?" Anna asked.

"They'll dance again, then cut to five finalists. The winner will be announced later tonight."

A bank of lights came on, holding off the darkness. When the drumbeat and chanting from the center of the arena began once more, the costumed warriors resumed their dance.

In the stark artificial light, Dusty's features were sharply defined by light and shadow. She stared, for she had never realized how deep the dimples in his cheeks were, or that there was a slight cleft in his chin. His long lashes cast strokes of shade across his cheeks. She frowned. No wonder it was impossible to ignore him—he was just too gorgeous!

As the second dance continued, she became so involved with the spectacle and her thoughts that she lost track of time. The next thing she knew, the world was quiet and the contestants were walking off the performing area. "What happened?" she asked Sue. "Did they choose the finalists?"

Sue was feeding her baby a bottle. "I wondered if you had zoned out. Yes, and Dusty made it."

Anna's cheeks flamed. Was her preoccupation with him that obvious? "That's nice . . ."

Sue smiled knowingly. "I figured you might think so. Can you stay to see them announce the winners? That'll probably be around midnight."

Anna shook her head, getting to her feet. "I just dropped by to give someone a message. Thanks for your help."

Sue nodded. "No problem. Is Dusty who you're looking for?"

Anna blanched. The last thing she wanted was this woman to tell Dusty how she'd reacted to his performance. "Uh, no," she lied.

Sue's expression was a mixture of skepticism and sympathy. But she didn't press Anna. Instead she nodded and said, "Oh. Well, maybe I'll see you next year. These powwows are like family reunions for us."

Anna could barely manage a smile. She doubted she'd be in any position to come to a powwow in Tahlequah next year. Especially with Dusty Dare. She was sad as she scanned the park, which was teeming with people bound by heritage and blood. How she envied them this chance to get together every year and renew old friendships. Her stepfather had died twelve years ago of a stroke, her mother, a year later of complications from influenza. Uncle Bud and Steven were the only family she had. Not much call for family reunions. Of course, right now she *could* use a reunion—with her wayward brother.

After only a few paces, she spotted Dusty Dare making his way through the benches where a crowd had gathered to congratulate the finalists. As she watched, he paused and accepted a paper cup from a long-haired boy in jeans and a Garth Brooks T-shirt. Dusty drank, patted the boy's shoulder and handed him back the cup. He walked on, only to be stopped by several more well-wishers.

Anna didn't want to interrupt, so she stood apart from the group, hoping he'd see her. It was dark where she was, since Dusty and his little band of admirers were well outside the halo of the lighted arena. The master of ceremonies announced the Eagle Dance. She heard drums begin again and glanced over to see it getting under way. It looked interesting, but this wasn't really the time to sightsee. She'd come to find her boss, and now that she had, she'd speak to him and leave. He laughed, a rich sound that warmed something deep inside her.

From time to time he spoke in a language she didn't understand but she assumed it was Cherokee. Screwing up her nerve, she started forward, and her movement caught his attention. He was in midsentence when their gazes met, and he didn't finish. The silence was so sudden and so long that everybody turned toward her.

"Uh, Mr. Dare?" she asked hesitantly. "May I talk to you—in, uh, private?"

His expression a mix of surprise and wariness, he excused himself to his admirers and sauntered toward her, accompanied by the jingling of bells. "I thought you were going to bed early," he said once they were alone beside a crooked old oak. A lighted hot-dog stand ten feet away gave off enough illumination for Anna to see that he was curious.

He seemed somehow taller, broader. And at close range, the explosion of ceremonial plumage that fluttered about him in the evening breeze was even more impressive—like some rare bird of prey.

"If you say 'how' to me, you're fired," Dusty warned, pulling her from her thoughts.

She frowned in confusion. "How, what?"

"Just how! Most non-Indians I meet say that when I'm dressed like this. But real Indians don't greet each other that way."

She was irked by his assumption that she would be so insensitive. "I'm from Oklahoma, remember? I grew up with Indians. I never said 'how' to any of them, except in chemistry when I asked Roger Young Thunder how to make an electromagnet." She lifted her chin. "I liked Roger, but then, he didn't constantly think the worst about me."

The yellow light was bright enough to reveal the amusement in his eyes. "Okay," he said, relenting, his expression almost pleasant. "So, you're politically correct. Congratulations."

Though he'd spoken casually, she heard a touch of pain in his statement and felt her anger dissipate. "I forgot. Max told me about all the fights you got into because of—"

"Max is an old man who talks too much," he interrupted, his tone making it clear he didn't intend to discuss his youth. "Why are you here, Miss Andrews?"

He was too near, and the breeze was plaguing her with his scent. Deciding to just get on with things, she said hurriedly, "When I called Thad tonight he had great news."

At the mention of Thad's name, all pleasantness left his face, but she continued, "He said Steven had been in Dallas with an old girlfriend, and she gave him your message about not prosecuting."

He inclined his head. "And?"

She shrugged, embarrassed, wishing she had more concrete news. "Well, he left her house, but I'm sure he's on his way back here."

Dusty pursed his lips and said, "That is good news." The remark held little inflection. Their eyes met, and Anna felt an odd mix of emotions. "Did you watch me dance?" he asked, suddenly.

Her cheeks went hot and she was glad for the cover of darkness. "Yes. You were . . . colorful."

"I was supposed to look bloodthirsty," he said, sounding vaguely amused.

"You *always* look bloodthirsty."

"Wasn't I worse with all this war paint?" He pretended disappointment.

She heard the laughter in his tone, but somehow she didn't mind. She shook her head, fighting an urge to smile. "Nope. I was no more terrified than usual."

He flashed a quick grin and teased, "Well, as long as you were terrified. Are you staying to watch the rest of the contests?"

She stuffed her hands into her pockets, wanting badly to ask if he would perform again. She'd love to see that. His war dance was almost as exciting as his kiss. But she decided that spending too much time in the dark with Dusty wasn't going to do her peace of mind any good. He was simply too dangerous. "I don't think so," she murmured, hoping her reluctance wasn't evident in her voice. "Five o'clock comes early." She couldn't help but ask, "What time will this all end?"

"Two. Four." He shrugged, his face unreadable. "We don't run powwows by a clock." Anna's attention was diverted when a wayward breeze rippled his loincloth. All of a sudden she was too preoccupied to come up with a single sensible reply. It took her several seconds to realize Dusty was chuckling. "Would you like me to turn around, or can you see enough?"

His humor-filled question woke her from her reverie. Dismayed, she realized she'd been staring at his bare hip, which had been exposed by the wind.

Her gaze flew to his, and she could see that he was entirely too pleased with himself. Drat! He probably had the mistaken idea she thought he was sexy or something!

She opened her mouth but was unable to form any words—which was probably just as well, because anything she might have said in her defense would have been a lie.

FOR DUSTY DARE, cutting cattle was a diversion, a rich man's hobby that could net millions of dollars if invested in the right horses. For Anna, it was a dust-eating way of life. Cutting was a ranch chore, necessary to sort individual animals from the herd for various reasons. Cattle had a natural herding instinct that caused them to bunch together and avoid being singled out.

But not every horse was up to the task. A cutting horse had to be lightning quick, turn on a button and smart enough to predict a cow's escape plan.

Anna patted her horse's neck fondly. Lady Freckle Handy had all those talents, and with the right training Anna thought the three-year-old could become a world champion. But first she had to win some small competitions, such as this one. Anna's insides twisted at the reminder of her own test.

From atop Freckle's back, she anxiously scanned the sunny arena for a tall man in a black straw Stetson. He'd come by earlier to check on the horses and had introduced her to his two older cousins, Lou and Ed, and Lou's son, Jerry. He hadn't lingered, though. Instead, he'd gone off to watch the other competitions. She'd seen him occasionally mingling with the crowd, but couldn't locate him right now in the undulating sea of cowboy hats.

The woods to the right of the arena were as green and rich as velvet on this bright June day. Oak and cottonwood leaves rustled and wagged in the warm afternoon breeze. Pulling her own tan Stetson lower on her brow, she swung her gaze to the parking lot on her left, still not finding Dusty. Beyond the parking lot stood the little motel where she'd spent a restless night, bothered by unwelcome dreams of a powerful man and his hot kisses.

Squelching the memory, she watched the arena before her as a buzzer sounded to end another cutting. There was moderate applause being offered for a moderate success. The contestant's passable score was called out, and Anna gulped, trying not to think about what she was about to do. One more contestant, then it would be her turn.

She could hear drums in the distance. Apparently the powwow was continuing today. She wondered how Dusty had done. He hadn't mentioned the competition, and in her nervousness, she'd forgotten to ask.

Trying to quell a new bout of nerves, she inhaled deeply. Along with the scent of dust in the warm air, she could detect the spicy smell of burritos and barbecue drifting across from the concession wagon. The odor made her feel nauseated. She shifted in the saddle, trying to calm herself. Transferring her nervousness to Freckle could be disastrous. A fretful horse was likely to make mistakes, and Anna couldn't afford that, not if she was to prove her worth as a trainer.

She had warmed up her mare, so Freckle was ready, and in about a minute, their test would begin.

"Go for the white heifer with the dark forelegs."

Anna almost fell out of the saddle from the shock of hearing Dusty's voice so close by. She twisted to look at him. "What?"

Squinting up at her, he adjusted his hat to block out the blinding sun that was directly above Anna's head. He was dressed in a red, starched, button-down shirt, black jeans with a knife-sharp crease, custom-fitted black chaps, boots and silver spurs. And he looked wonderful.

"I've been watching, and the milky heifer with the black forelegs hasn't been worked," he said. "She'll be fresh, which will give Freckle a good challenge. For your second cut, corral that black-eyed white-face standing in the center. Let Freckle move in close. You know she's chargey, so she'll want to, anyway."

Anna nodded, but didn't have time to say anything before he took her hand in his and gave it a squeeze. "Good luck," he murmured. Then he left to mount his turnback horse. He would be in the ring with her, keeping the cow being worked from escaping to the far end of the arena.

His relatives would be helping, too. Ed would be another turnback rider, while Lou and Jerry worked as herd holders. As herd holders, their job was to keep the other cattle bunched at the back of the arena after one cow had been separated.

As the buzzer sounded for the cutter just ahead of her, Anna swallowed nervous bile, flexing the hand Dusty had squeezed. It seemed unusually warm. She forced herself to focus. This was it—she couldn't fall apart now.

The other cutter's score was announced, and the applause was loud. Good score. Not unbeatable, but good. Anna felt in her heart that Freckle could top any horse here. There was no reason for the mare to lose. Unless Anna did something to mess things up—like stiffen in the saddle, or take her eye off the cow, or lose her balance and fall. No.

She never fell. Well, not in years. Not since she was nine. It was just that she wanted so badly to show Dusty that she was a good trainer. She wanted to see him proud of her. Just once.

Concentrating, she relaxed her shoulders and legs and eased back in the saddle until she was in a classic cutter's slump. She could do this. It was no different than any other working day for her. She'd spent most of her life training cutting horses. If only she could forget that more than her pride was at stake.

Twenty cows were herded to the far end of the arena, as Anna was signaled to enter. Dusty and his cousins were mounted and in place—Lou and Jerry in front of the bunched cattle, Ed closer on her right, Dusty on her left. Anna walked Freckle along the center of the ring toward the herd. When she crossed a line about thirty feet from the herd, the clock started running. She now had two and a half minutes to showcase Freckle.

She scanned the cows until she saw the white heifer with the dark forelegs. Slowly, gently, she led Freckle deep into the herd. The whole arena had gone still, with only the occasional bawl of a cow, murmur from the bleachers or squeak of saddle leather breaking the stillness. Cutting was quiet work. It had to be, otherwise the cows could be spooked. She could almost hear her own heart beating as she began to drive the white heifer and six others out of the herd.

The separated cows milled about, trying to stay together despite their agitation. Anna maneuvered Freckle through the smaller herd until the milky heifer Dusty had suggested she work was in front of her. With a final silent prayer, she lowered her rein hand, the signal for Freckle to start. The mare instantly dropped her head and took charge.

Wanting desperately to get back to the herd, the little cow darted left and right, and Freckle anticipated the movements, blocking with a rapid two-step to one side and then the other.

Not easily thwarted, the heifer dodged left again, but Freckle matched her. As the cow lurched the other way, Freckle swung around to stop her, again stepping from side to side. Warming to the game like a puppy with a new ball, the mare sank low to the ground, her hooves dancing to and fro, backward and forward to keep the cow contained.

It was Anna's job to stay in her seat and be loose enough to flow with the horse's sudden moves. She could feel her cutting saddle beneath her floating left and right, forward and backward, as the horse continued her sambalike moves around the center of the ring, preventing the cow's escape at every turn.

Anna's rein hand was low and loose, while her other hand gripped the saddle horn to help her keep her balance. She thought Freckle had done a good job so far and wanted to laugh, but she couldn't. She had to remain focused—this ride wasn't over yet.

The heifer bolted left, and Anna had to concentrate to stay in the saddle while applying slight pressure in the right stirrup. The cow stopped and launched herself in the opposite direction. Anna maintained her deep seat as Freckle rose in the air and shifted right. Automatically Anna applied pressure in the left stirrup, her eyes never leaving the cow.

She told herself to stay glued to the saddle, no matter how sharp a turn her horse might make. That was her job, and she wasn't about to screw it up. Not with Dusty Dare watching for the slightest mistake. She hunkered low, focusing totally as the horse zigged and zagged and lurched beneath her, anticipating and frustrating the heifer.

Then the cow simply gave up and turned away, going completely still. Anna lifted her rein hand to signal Freckle off the cow. She heard someone shout, "Twenty-five seconds," and knew it was Dusty telling her how much time she had left.

It was always better to be working a cow when the buzzer went off than to "die in the herd," so she headed back toward the bunched cattle, trying to remain calm. She covertly checked her reins to be sure they hadn't tangled. Seeing that everything was fine, she took a deep breath, inhaling dust. She could feel the sweaty heat rising off her horse, and somehow the familiarity of it all relaxed her. Reaching the herd, she separated two calves. There was little time left.

The heifer with the black eye turned and stared at her, and Anna knew that Dusty had been right to suggest she work this one, too. With her free hand on the saddle horn, she signaled Freckle to separate the heifer further from the herd. The second calf slipped away and melted back to join the rest of the cattle.

Just as she lowered her rein hand, the heifer started to bolt toward Dusty. But Freckle was ready, and she bolted, too, blocking the cow's escape. Anna heard, "Ten seconds," but she didn't take her eyes from the cow.

Freckle was eager and fairly quivered with excitement. They moved back and forth, she and her horse, like one fluid being. The experience was exhilarating. Anna had never ridden such a wonderful cutter. Her movements were efficient and economical; there was no chargeyness in her now. Not a speck. Freckle was perfect, reacting like a champion. In the two weeks since Anna had taken over her training, the horse had improved a hundred percent. Anna wanted to cry with joy. Being on this horse was an adventure she'd never tire of. She knew in her heart that one day

Freckle would win cutting's Triple Crown. Another million-dollar champion for Bent River.

The buzzer sounded just as the black-eyed cow gave up, and there was a loud burst of applause that lasted until Freckle's score was announced. It was a great score. Possibly a winning score! Anna rode the mare from the arena amid wild cheers from the crowd. They knew a champion in the making when they saw one.

When Anna dismounted, she hugged Freckle's neck, murmuring endearments. Out of the corner of her eye, she caught a flash of red coming toward her, and her heart went to her throat. She turned, but her vision was blurry so she couldn't see Dusty clearly. Then she realized that she was crying. Joy surging through her, she leapt into his arms. "Dusty! Dusty! What a wonderful horse!"

Then with no thought to the consequences, she kissed him.

CHAPTER NINE

FOR A SECOND, Anna hung in midair, clinging to his neck. His lack of reaction made it plain that her kiss had caught him by surprise. But he recovered quickly, wrapping his arms about her waist and returning the kiss.

Indescribable sensations sizzled through her as he held her against him, and the delight of victory over Freckle's performance became a delight of a very different kind. Fiery heat radiated from his lips and caressing hands. The low guttural sound that came from his throat as he moved his lips across hers told her he was affected in a way that had nothing to do with contests or horses.

All too soon the kiss was over, and she was set firmly down on her feet, although Dusty's hands lingered at her waist. She stared into his eyes, his features swimming before her as she tried to refocus on a world devoid of the dazzling stimulation of his kiss.

It was only when she became aware of the snickering around them that she realized the full implication of what she'd done.

She knew she must be blushing fiercely, because her face burned. "Oh! I'm . . ." Clutching her hands together, she made a brave effort to smile despite her embarrassment. "It's just that I was so excited about Freckle I lost my head," she explained in a breathy voice, trying to convince herself that it was the whole truth.

His smile made her heart ache for the touch of his lips on hers. She resisted the urge to stroke his rugged cheek. Her momentary rashness could be explained, but there was no excuse for any further physical contact.

He bent to retrieve something, and Anna realized her hat had fallen to the dirt when she'd so inelegantly pounced on him.

He held the hat in her direction. "Congratulations," he said, as if nothing had happened.

Swallowing to ease the tenseness in her throat, she asked weakly, "Did I pass?"

His gaze lingered on her face, where tendrils of hair had fallen from her braid. "I'd say you passed all right, sugar."

Her breath caught, for his double meaning was brazenly clear in the huskiness of his tone. He knew excitement about Freckle's performance wasn't the only reason for her actions. Not wanting to dwell on that, she grabbed her hat from his hand and spun away. "Freckle isn't the only one around here who needs hosing down," she muttered. Then she caught the mare's reins and stalked off.

His low-pitched chuckle chased after her, wordlessly implying that she might need cooling off, too.

ANNA SHOWERED and changed into clean jeans and a rose-colored tank top. She was about to head back to the arena to watch more cuttings when the ringing of her phone stopped her.

"Hello?"

"Sweetie? It's Thad."

Anna frowned, suddenly worried. "What's wrong? You sound upset."

There was an uneasy pause, and she thought she'd better sit down. Perching on the bed, she asked, "What's the matter, Thad?"

"There's been a fire at your ranch," he said. "I'm afraid your house is gone. And, uh, your uncle..."

"Uncle Bud? Is he okay?"

"He managed to get out a window, but, well—" Thad cleared his throat "—he's in St. John's Hospital, in Tulsa. Mainly for smoke inhalation."

"Oh, my Lord!" Anna cried. "I'll be there as soon as I can."

"I'll stay here at the hospital until you get here."

"Thank you. You're a lifesaver," she said before hanging up.

When she found him, Dusty insisted on taking her to Tulsa immediately, even though the cuttings were still going on in the three-year-old class, and the winner wouldn't be announced for another hour. He also made arrangements with Ed to get the horses back to Bent River.

Anna sat in apprehensive silence during the whole trip back. When Dusty pulled into the hospital parking lot, she asked, "Did you want to come up? If not, Thad can give me a ride back."

He looked over at her, frowning. "No, I won't come up. I've got some business to take care of. So, you'd better let Thad give you a lift back."

Stung by his dismissal, she hopped out of the truck and dashed through the double doors of the hospital, trying to believe that he wasn't really uncaring. But hadn't she always known he was the sort of man whose own interests came first? Typical, she groused inwardly, wondering why his lack of concern hurt her so much.

As she sprinted along the white-tiled corridor toward the bank of elevators, she made a grim vow. This was absolutely the end of any silly fantasies about that self-centered cowboy. Thad was the man for her. He was dependable and trustworthy. Even though Thad had only met Uncle Bud a few times, he was here.

ANNA YAWNED and was sorry she'd chosen that exact second to do so, for just as her mouth opened Thad leaned across the front seat of his car to kiss her good-night. "Oh," she said sheepishly. "Sorry. It's just that I'm worn out."

"That's okay. It is late. Nearly midnight." He pecked her cheek. "Good night, sweetie. I'm glad Bud's going to be okay. Call me tomorrow and let me know how he's doing."

She nodded, yawned again. "You were great to stay the whole time." Smiling, she slipped out the passenger door and waved as he drove away.

Taking only a few steps in the direction of her cottage, she remembered she needed to fetch some invoices from Dusty's den. When she got there, she was surprised to find him sitting behind his desk. "Oh. Sorry. I didn't mean to disturb you. I came for the farrier and saddle-repair bills."

"No problem," he said, standing. "I was just leaving." Picking up a stack of papers, he handed them to her. "Here they are, plus a few more I've gone over."

He seemed preoccupied, and she wondered why. "Thanks," she said. "And good night."

She turned to go, but he stopped her. "How's your uncle?"

She managed a small smile. "He's fine, considering. They figure he'll be in the hospital a week—if he continues to do well."

Dusty nodded, but didn't smile. "That's good."

She watched him for a second, again trying to figure out what was troubling him. Then she had a frightening thought. "Is something wrong with Freckle?"

He stared at her, his face registering puzzlement, then he shook his head. "No. She's fine. Ed brought her back an hour ago. He said she won. You should be proud."

Anna's relieved smile was genuine. "She's a great horse. I had a feeling she'd win."

He nodded, then frowned as his mind seemed to return to some bleak thought. Anna's smile died, too. "Anything wrong?" she asked. "Did you lose the dance thing?"

"The dance—" Then understanding apparently hit him. "No, I didn't lose."

He must have thought he read surprise on her face for he asked, "Is that so unbelievable?"

"No, you were fantastic!" she blurted, then bit her lip, wishing she hadn't been quite so gushy. He might take it wrong. She clutched the papers to her chest. "You should be proud, too."

He nodded, his half smile hardly cheerful. "Thanks."

She shifted uncomfortably, not sure what was going on with him, but positive he wasn't going to share it with her. "Good night, then," she said.

He nodded distractedly, his attention already elsewhere.

She left the house feeling strangely deflated. Although he seemed to have mellowed in his original opinion of her abilities, he would always see her as the sister of a thief. And he could still put her brother in jail and take away her home. Not that much was left of it—a scorched barn, some frightened horses and goats, and a pile of ashes where her house had stood.

Thank heaven Euby Hobbs had seen the smoke and brought his hands over to find her uncle, hose down the barn and rescue her livestock. She'd spoken with Euby this evening, and they'd worked out a deal where he'd care for her livestock, instead of paying his training fees for a while.

She exhaled sadly. To Dusty, her family troubles were her own concern. He obviously didn't think they affected him, except as far as the return of his property was concerned. He hadn't even asked about her house.

A few nights later, Anna slipped into Dusty's office to leave some cost figures and purchase orders he wanted to go over before he left for work the next morning. It was very late, because she'd gone into town to visit her uncle, who, thankfully, was still improving.

The den was dark and the house silent, which was no surprise, since it was after eleven. On her way out of the office, she heard a commotion coming from upstairs. There was a female squeal, followed quickly by a rapid thudding. Worried, she rushed toward the staircase, hoping no one had fallen down it.

When she reached the foyer, she saw Dusty descending the long curving staircase holding a wriggling and squealing bundle encased in a bed sheet.

Anna found herself watching openmouthed as she recognized the whining voice as Nicole's.

When Dusty halted at the bottom of the steps, he deposited his niece on her feet. His features were set in both concern and irritation. He shook his head, seeming at a loss. "Look, Nicole, you can't go around surprising men with candlelight snacks in their bedrooms, wearing—" he ran his hands roughly through his hair "—whatever that is you've got on under that sheet."

"It's a teddy and—"

"I don't want to know," he cut in, his voice gruff with frustration. "Just...just don't do it again, okay?"

"But Dusty," she wailed, struggling from the sheet to reach for him and baring one shoulder. "I love you. Don't you love me...a little?"

"Nicole," Dusty said sternly. "I'm afraid you've mistaken kindness for something else. I'm your uncle. Maybe just by marriage, but I have no intention of being anything more than that to you."

The girl stumbled back a step, her face screwing up in anguish. "But I'll never love anybody else!"

Mouthing a curse, he patted her covered shoulder. "Yes, you will," he assured her. Firmly turning her away, he gave her a nudge between the shoulder blades in the direction of her room. "Now go to bed, young lady, and we'll forget this."

"You think I'm just a kid!" she cried, wheeling back. When she did, her eyes widened, and Anna realized she'd been spotted. She felt badly for the child, having her humiliation witnessed, but she didn't speak and couldn't move.

"I think," Dusty said thinly, "you're a lovely girl who's been watching too much TV."

With a heart wrenching sob, Nicole gathered the sheet about her and made an ungainly, loping getaway down the hall. After a few seconds, her footfalls died away and a door slammed.

Anna remained frozen, staring at Dusty's bare chest. He looked tousled and shaken by the incident. She'd never seen him so disconcerted before. He was always completely in control, and this glimpse at the vulnerable side of him was endearing.

As he turned to go back upstairs, he noticed her standing there and sent an exasperated glance toward heaven. "Good evening, Miss Andrews. Did you want to talk to me, or are you here for the late show?"

She shook her head and stepped out of the shadows. "I'm sorry. I didn't mean to eavesdrop. I left those papers you wanted in your—"

"Fine. I'll see you tomorrow," he broke in, dismissing her, and started up the steps.

He looked so grave, so upset, Anna's heart went out to him. "Maybe she needs a hobby," she offered quietly.

"She needs a spanking."

"I'll talk to her—explain the term 'jailbait.'" She shrugged, adding more to herself than to him, "I'd meant to have a talk with her, anyway."

He stopped on the stairs and eyed her. "Why do I suddenly get the feeling it was Nicole who was spying on me at the pool that night?"

The vision of his nude body rushed through her mind, and she became strangely tongue-tied.

"Why didn't you tell me, Miss Andrews?"

Her gaze flitted around the big entryway. Didn't he remember? Instead of giving her time to explain, he'd tugged her into his arms and planted a bruising, breathtaking kiss on her.

Anna's silence was answer enough, it seemed, because he chuckled bitterly. "Hell, I'm sorry," he said, sounding disgusted. "I should have known."

She was startled by the regret in his voice. "Apology accepted."

Their glances met, and Anna grew self-conscious beneath his stare. Time passed, or possibly it stood still—she couldn't be sure. Somewhere along the way, though, the message in his expression changed from apology to attraction and promise. *Let me make love to you,* it seemed to say. She feared he could detect the struggle her body was having with her brain.

Swallowing hard, she somehow managed to control her emotions and began to edge around him in a wide arc, frightened that if she got too close, she wouldn't be able to resist the temptation in his eyes. "You . . . you handled that thing with Nicole pretty well,'' she offered in the pitiful hope that inanities would blot out her wayward desires.

He smiled a humorless smile. "I could tell by the sobbing."

"You have to understand," she said, concentrating more on her escape route than her words, "being rejected by someone when you've offered yourself to them is terribly painful."

A shadow passed across his features, but he maintained his show of teeth. "Really?" Though that one word was uttered casually, there was a steel-edged irony in his tone, and Anna winced at the subtle reminder that he'd just been rejected—by her. Not knowing how to reply to that, she simply turned and fled.

ANNA HAD BEEN TRAINING Freckle to take tighter turns, and the mare was lathered and tired. While the horse rested for a moment, she glanced around and was startled to see Nicole lurking nearby. Sensing the girl wasn't there by accident, she walked Freckle over.

She hadn't seen her at all on Sunday. According to Max, she'd said she was sick and stayed in her room. Poor kid. Anna knew what Nicole's problem had really been. Rejection was hard at any age, but at fifteen . . .

"Hi, Nicole," she ventured. "How'd you like to ride Freckle if I hold the reins and walk her. She needs to cool off, and you ought to get used to being up on a horse if you're going to live on a ranch."

Nicole sent a brief angst-ridden glance Anna's way. She looked bad—red puffy eyes and lank dull hair. She clearly hadn't slept much. Anna dismounted and looped the mare's reins over the top rail, then climbed the pole fence and jumped down to the other side. "Come on. It'll take your mind off . . . things."

The girl had been toying with a button on her green shirt, acting completely disinterested, but Anna wasn't fooled. Nicole was down here for a reason, and it wasn't her love for horses. It was painfully apparent that she wanted to talk. And since her mother wasn't here, Anna supposed Nicole had decided she was the next best thing. Besides, she was already aware of the problem. Taking the girl's hand, Anna urged, "Come on. Freckle's real gentle. It'll be fun."

Anna was astonished when Nicole ran into her arms, practically knocking her over. "Oh, Anna, he hates me," she wailed forlornly against her shirt. "And I love him so much it hurts!"

Anna grimaced, feeling badly for the child. She hugged her and stroked her hair soothingly. "Now, now. It isn't as bad as all that. Dusty doesn't hate you, not even a little."

"But he does. You saw how he treated me. And I've loved him from the first second I saw him. He's so big and handsome, and he smells so good."

Anna gritted her teeth. There was a lot of that going around—Dusty seemed to affect women of all ages. She squelched the thought. "You don't really love him, Nicole," she insisted gently. "You just think you do. It's normal for a girl your age to have a crush on an older man. I loved a teacher once the very same way." She didn't go on to say that she'd never climbed into her teacher's bed, however.

Nicole lifted her head, her face a picture of agony. "But my mom's second husband was twenty years older than she was. Dusty's only twenty-one years older than me!"

Anna sighed. "Maybe so. But your mother wasn't fifteen, Nicole. Don't you know that a man could go to jail if he, er, got romantic with a girl your age?"

Nicole sniffed, looking through teary eyes. "Huh?"

Anna nodded, deciding the age thing was as good an excuse as any. "It's against the law for a man of Dusty's age to be intimately involved with a minor."

Nicole wiped her eyes with the back of her hand. "It is?"

"Yes. So, you can see why your uncle was upset. You were trying to make him break the law."

Nicole's eyes widened. "But I didn't mean it. I just wanted him to know I loved him."

Anna smiled reassuringly, smoothing the girl's long hair through her fingers, trying to untangle it. "Maybe it would be better if you had a hobby to take your mind off your uncle. It's clear that the goats and your kitten aren't enough to keep you occupied. And you don't seem to like the horses."

Nicole sniffed again and shook her head. "Horses stink." She ran a hand through her hair, frowning thoughtfully. "I like music. Mom said I could maybe take lessons sometime."

Anna nodded. "Sounds good. Singing? An instrument? What sort of lessons?"

Nicole shrugged. "I'm not sure."

"Tell you what—why don't you and I walk Freckle, then I'll get her groomed while you go clean up. After that, we can drive into Tulsa and check out a music store I know of. They rent instruments and hold classes." Motioning for Nicole to follow, she climbed the fence. When they were inside the pen, Nicole walked beside Anna as she cooled down Freckle.

"So, how old do I have to be to date Uncle Dusty and not send him to jail?" Nicole asked after a few minutes.

Anna shook her head helplessly. This was one stubborn girl. "Eighteen, I'm afraid."

"Eighteen?" Nicole echoed. "I just turned fifteen last month. Bummer." She kicked at the dirt with her combat boot. "Do you think he'd wait for me? He's so cute and all."

Anna chewed the inside of her cheek. It was plain that Dusty's problem with Nicole wasn't easily solved. But it was very likely, considering the fickleness of teenage girls, that in the next three years, Nicole would get over her crush and find someone nearer her own age. "I can't speak for him," she said, choosing her words carefully. She couldn't make this girl any promises, and she doubted that Dusty was in the habit of waiting for anything. "I always try to think of the future this way. If something's meant to be, it'll be. No sense in sweating it."

"Anna?" Nicole asked. "Don't you think Dusty's a hunk and a half? I mean, isn't he the most totally doable stud muffin you've ever seen?"

"Totally doable studmuffin?" Anna repeated. "Where in the world do you pick up language like that? Do you even know what it means?"

"Sure, it means—"

"Never mind," she said with a laugh. "And to answer your question, I think Mr. Dare is a perfectly average man." It was an utter lie, which was too bad, because she'd have given anything to mean it.

CHAPTER TEN

THAT NIGHT, Anna had to venture back to the main house to talk to Dusty about some estimates for fence repairs, although she'd have rather jumped off a cliff into a cactus patch. It had been two days since their encounter in the entryway, but somehow it didn't seem like two seconds. And, here she was, standing at his office door, expected—and late.

He looked up from his reading and gave her a where-have-you-been frown. "Come in," he said, with a curt nod toward what she'd come to think of as the punishment chair.

She took her seat, deciding not to explain her lateness, since her reluctance to face him was the only reason. He probably already knew that, anyway. Instead, she reached across the desk and handed him the papers. "Boomer Fencing's bid is the lowest, but I'm not sure we should go that route. You'll see by my notes—"

"Just sit. I'll take a look," he said gruffly.

With a fresh stab of unease, she sat back, clutching the chair arms.

He was silent for a long time. Maybe a month. At least that was how it seemed to Anna. When she'd entered, his gaze had held none of the sensuality she'd seen two nights ago. Tonight he radiated anger and some tightly controlled emotion she couldn't read.

She glanced at her white-knuckled hands. Not wanting him to see her apprehension, she peeled them off the chair arms and balled them into fists in her lap. Then, unable to help herself, her mind slid treacherously back to Saturday night—Dusty standing at the bottom of the stairs and poor, misguided Nicole... "I talked to her," she said, then realized she'd spoken aloud.

He looked perplexed. "What?"

Stupid! she berated herself. *Why would you want to remind him of the other night!* Flushing, she shrugged. "I had that talk with Nicole and..." The sentence faded away in her self-consciousness.

He watched her silently, his jaw knotting and unknotting with measured regularity. She couldn't tell if he was irritated by the memory of that night or merely the interruption of his reading. "I appreciate it," he murmured, dropping his gaze to the pages in his hand.

She slumped back, not knowing if she was relieved or hurt by the lack of attraction in his eyes. With a deep breath, she decided it was better this way. Better to have ignored her desires and never made love to him. Her mother was right about his type.

"We'll go with Randolf Pole Barn and Fence Company." He indicated her notations with a tap of his finger bringing her back to the present. "You're right. He's not the lowest bid, but the quality's there."

Anna relaxed slightly, but when she didn't leave immediately he asked, "Anything else?"

Apparently he'd expected her to hop up, bark, "Yes, sir!" and go. She stood belatedly, leaning forward to retrieve the papers. "No... sir. I'll call Randall's in the morning." She got up and made it to the door before a thought occurred to her. "Uh, Mr.—"

The ringing of his phone stilled her. He picked up the receiver. "Dare, here." Anna vacillated between not wanting to eavesdrop on his conversation and wanting to ask him question that had been bothering her since Freckle had won on Saturday. So she stood there. Dusty knew she was listening. If the conversation was private, he'd signal her to leave.

"Yes, hello, Sar—" He stopped himself, swiveling his chair around so that his back was to Anna. "Go ahead," he continued quietly.

Anna grew curious at his strange behavior and stealthily slipped closer to hear. "I see," he was saying. "Thank you for getting back to me so quickly. I'll be in touch."

He hung up slowly and seemed to Anna to be deep in unpleasant thoughts. She scurried noiselessly toward the door, feeling a twinge of guilt for spying. She waited, but he never moved. After he'd sat there for a long time, his fist still on the receiver, Anna asked, "Bad news?"

His head snapped up. Clearly he'd forgotten her presence. How flattering. "Nothing. Business. Uh, what did you want?"

She felt awkward, not wanting to trouble him when it was obvious there was something very wrong. "I...well, it's not that important. I can come back tomorrow."

He inhaled as though working to relax. "Miss Andrews, if there's a problem, tell me."

She leaned against the doorjamb. "It was just that I was wondering something."

He sat back in his leather chair, his glance steady, yet guarded. "Wondering what?"

Her heart pounded. She wanted to ask him another question, but decided to begin with a more innocent one. "I was wondering how the interviewing for a new stable manager's going. I understand you've gotten some résumés."

He lifted a shoulder. "Quite a few, but none with the qualifications I'd like."

She nodded, trying to get up her nerve to ask the other question.

"I gave Frosty Fremont a call last week," he said when she made no comment.

In fact, she had been about to speak, but his words struck her momentarily dumb. "Frosty Fremont?" she managed finally. "Why, a couple of the horses he's trained are in the NCHA Hall of Fame. You . . . you think you might be able to get him to work for you?"

Another nonchalant shrug. "I've heard rumors he's not happy at the Silver Q in Dallas, so I gave him a call. He's flying up next week to talk."

Anna swallowed, her airy fantasies of being allowed to stay here crashing to her feet. "I see," she said. "I'm surprised you hired Steven if you can get a man like Mr. Fremont to consider working for you."

"I talked to Frosty last year before I hired your brother, but he thought things would get better where he was. Your brother had won some competitions on horses that were only fair. He had talent, and I gambled." He steepled his hands. "I never made a bigger mistake before or since."

Anna flinched at his cruel remark, hurriedly reminding him, "You know, Steven and I had the same teacher. I think Uncle Bud would have been as great as Frosty Fremont if he hadn't gotten hurt in that freak fall."

Dusty pursed his lips. "It's possible."

With her heart pounding in her ears, she forced herself to go ahead and ask what she really wanted to know. "How do you think I'm doing as manager? Not that I'm fishing for compliments," she added apprehensively. "I only wanted to know your opinion, since you never say much."

He crossed his arms. She couldn't tell if his expression was of contemplation or displeasure. Fearing the worst, she dropped her gaze.

"You're capable," he admitted, "but you still have a great deal to learn."

The tepid answer didn't sit well with Anna, and her feelings must have shown in her expression, for his lips twitched upward in a weary smile. "Don't take it to heart, Miss Andrews. Brett and I have one of the best stables in Oklahoma, simply because our standards are impossibly high."

Deep resentment washed over her. "What about Freckle? Don't you think she improved with my training?"

"I admit you surprised me. But since you're working with some of the best horses in the country, who can say where the credit belongs? Can you swear it was you and not the innate ability of the horse?" He paused, his smile indulgent. "Don't be impatient. Give yourself another five years to get seasoned—"

"Please," she snapped, her pride getting the better of her. "Don't patronize me. It's obvious that, because of what Steven did, you'll never think of me as worthwhile."

Dusty's features became hard with offense. "My feelings for you have nothing to do with your brother," he said, his voice rough. *Now* his eyes sparked with desire, but it was so unexpected that Anna sagged against the jamb. She could hardly catch her breath.

"Don't look at me that way," she cried. "I know that look, and I know the kind of man you are. The answer is no. No quickie affairs for me." She bit her lip as his gaze narrowed. "I have a wonderful boyfriend who would do anything for me, and I'm not interested in playing sex games with...with any self-centered Tom, Dick or—"

"Dusty?" he finished for her, his tone grim, almost hurt. He planted both palms on his desk and rose to his feet. "Thanks for clearing that up. But for the record, I'm not a type, Miss Andrews. I'm a man." Rounding the desk, he strode toward her, looking like some wild wounded thing, dangerous, yet thrilling. She cowered against the door-jamb.

When he was six inches away from her, he stopped, placing one hand on the wall above her shoulder. He didn't quite touch her, but she could feel his radiant heat, almost taste his hovering mouth. "I think you're more interested in me than you care to admit," he drawled, his lips parted in wicked invitation. "Why don't we find out."

He moved the remaining six inches and brought his mouth down on hers. His kiss was surprisingly soft. She heard a whimper and knew it came from her as her body filled with passion and need. A languid warmth invaded her limbs, and she was instantly weak, instantly his.

Dusty's caressing hands made her fully aware of just how much of a man he was. Her trembling, willful arms disobeyed her orders to remain still and curled about his shoulders.

He nibbled her lower lip seductively, making her sigh with eagerness. Then she surprised herself by pressing impatiently against him and massaging his muscled back with wanton fingers—wishing his skin were bare to her touch, wishing hers was bare to his.

Without warning, he wrenched himself away, his breathing heavy. "Don't play if you can't pay, Miss Andrews," he growled huskily, stalking to his desk and unceremoniously sweeping it clear of all contents. She could only stare, held in the grip of a passion-induced daze.

"I could have you right here, right now, if I wanted to," he challenged, his eyes glittering with frustration and fury. "*You* may not like me, but your *body* does!" He pounded his fists on the desk, then, disgusted, strode from the room. "Give my regards to the boyfriend."

She remained by the door, devastated by his sensual assault and his anger, without even the power to follow hi departure with her eyes. His clipped footfalls echoed along the hardwood floor until they faded completely, leaving the vast house shrouded in silence.

She looked straight ahead, focusing on the jumble of papers and office equipment he'd shoved from his desk. The disconnected phone began to emit a high-pitched screech, and to her shocked mind, it sounded as if it was laughing at her.

THAD STOOD in Bent River's drive, helping her from his sports car. He must have noticed her sadness, for he squeezed her fingers gently. "Don't worry, sweetie. Pneumonia isn't uncommon in somebody your uncle's age. He'll be fine."

Anna sighed. "It's just that I thought he'd be out of the hospital. It's been seven days since the fire. And now they say he has pneumonia." Agitated, she played with her braid. "The problems never seem to end."

Thad put his arm about her shoulders and kissed her temple. "I know. You've had it rough. But on the bright side, hasn't that Mrs. Prin been a great help?"

Anna peered at him, confused. "Mrs. Prin?"

He hugged her to him. "The nurse's aide that volunteers at St. John's. She's gotten your uncle to eat better, and she's always so friendly. I'm surprised you haven't noticed."

Admittedly Anna had been preoccupied—probably with things she was better off forgetting. But now that Thad mentioned it, she recalled the woman. A redhead about her own age, who was divorced and trying to fill a lot of empty hours. She nodded. "Oh, sure. Linda was her name. Right?"

"Lydia," Thad corrected. "Would you like to take a walk? I don't have to be back at the hotel right away."

Anna nodded, sliding her arm about his waist. "Sure. We haven't been able to be alone much these past weeks. Let's walk down by the pond."

They strolled in silence, skirting the house and the pool. Dusty had held a party there the night before, but she hadn't been included. She'd been told it was to celebrate the expansion of Cherokee Natural Gas. According to Max, Dusty was about to close a deal to buy out a Texas pipeline firm. Anyway, these folks didn't ride, so there'd been no need to include Anna. She told herself she was happy about that. The less time she spent around her boss the better.

Anna and Thad followed a path through the woods to a field where the grass grew tall and wildflowers proliferated. After another minute they crested a rise, then headed into a valley. In its center was a small pond blanketed with lily pads and surrounded by tall sycamores.

The night smelled of aromatic grasses, primrose and the sweet pungency of sycamore leaves. They wandered along the bank with their arms entwined about each other. There was rain somewhere in the distance—Anna could smell it on the breeze.

A fish jumping made a plopping sound in the darkness, and an orchestra of crickets played their night symphony, gentling Anna's troubled spirit.

She glanced up. Clouds seemed bent on scurrying one after the other over the moon, occasionally cloaking her and Thad in absolute darkness. It was during one of these moments that Thad surprised her with a kiss. She was completely unaffected by it and was glad he couldn't see her face.

She'd tried hard to remember her mother's warnings about fireworks men, and she'd fought her desire for Dusty hard. But lately she'd begun to wonder if her father hadn't simply been a jerk. Perhaps being a fireworks man wasn't necessarily a bad thing. And just because a man was nice and hardworking didn't necessarily make him the right husband for her.

Since Dusty's last kiss, she'd started to think that a certain amount of wild passion was essential to a relationship. She couldn't deny that kindness was important, too. But couldn't a person find both?

With Thad holding her in his arms and her lips still damp from his kiss, she felt more dissatisfaction than pleasure—not to mention more confusion. "Thad, I—"

"Anna, don't interrupt," he said hoarsely, pulling her to his chest. "I've been working up my courage for weeks, so don't stop me now." His tweedy blazer was rough against her cheek as he held her tightly to him. "I know we broke up partly because you love horses and always want them to be a part of your life, but—"

"Thad, I—"

"Anna, I can't let you go," he said bleakly. "I didn't tell you, but I've been offered a promotion in another city—San Francisco." She tried to speak, but he cut her off again. "No, it's okay. I turned it down. Told my boss I had to stay in Oklahoma, because the woman I love wouldn't be happy in California. What I'm saying is—" he squeezed her and inhaled as if to reinforce his courage "—I got a good raise and a promise that, when the Oklahoma City Elite Quadruplex becomes available, it's mine. It's a five-star hotel connected to a huge convention center. A real choice managership, sweetie. And it'll be mine in a year or so."

"That's wonderful, Thad. I had no idea."

"I know. I wanted it to be a surprise before I asked you to marry me . . . again. Please, say you will."

Anna could only stare at him. It wasn't that she was startled by his question. It was just that she'd thought she'd known what she would say when it came—yes. But now—

after being thoroughly thrown off balance by Dusty Dare—she wasn't sure any longer.

He cleared his throat. No, the sound hadn't come from Thad. They exchanged concerned glances. Coming to the same conclusion at the same instant, they turned in unison. The moon had popped out from behind a cloud, so the huge old sycamore nearby was no longer in darkness. To Anna's horror, a figure rose from a sitting position. "Dusty," she whispered, appalled.

His hands were on his hips, in a casual, almost insolent stance. "Anna, Thad," he said quietly, "didn't mean to intrude. I was just out...enjoying the silence. Seems Nicole's taken up the tuba."

Anna bit her lip. It hadn't been her fault Nicole had decided she wanted to learn to play the tuba. But she didn't try to defend herself; she had the feeling he didn't really care about that. It was unlike him to wander around the ranch late at night. Something else was wrong. Probably the same thing that had been bothering him last week.

He touched a finger to the brim of his hat and turned away to start toward the house. "Have a nice...walk."

Neither she nor Thad said anything. She supposed they both were too shocked and embarrassed to speak. They merely watched in silence as Dusty walked off into the night. When they could no longer see or hear him, Anna managed to look at Thad. It was only then that she realized they'd been holding each other the whole time. She pulled away.

"Damn," Thad said sullenly. "That guy *would* be out here now."

Anna shook her head, unaccountably sad and not daring to analyze it. "It's his land. I guess he can sit beside his own pond if he wants."

Thad shrugged, smiling weakly. "I guess. But I was hoping this would be private. You realize I just asked you to marry me, don't you?"

She nodded. "Yes, and I'm flattered. You're the nicest man I know."

"That's a good start." He hauled her into his arms, again, sighing against her forehead. "Oh, Anna, you don't know how I've dreamed of marrying you—having you live in the hotel with me. Two big rooms, with a southern exposure. And our apartment in the Quad in Oklahoma City'll be even better." He kissed her. "As far as your uncle's concerned, he can have a room at the Elite until you get your place rebuilt. Family rate," he teased. "He can move with us when we go, too, if he wants. We'll be a great team. I know we will."

"But... what about my work?"

He chuckled. "You won't have to work. I make good money."

"It's not the money, Thad. I love horses. I want to be around them."

He nuzzled her hair. "I know. I figure you could board a horse for riding on weekends. I want you to be happy."

Dejection coursed through her. The thought of living in town without grass or trees or the sweet smell of hay horrified her. And she didn't even want to imagine never training a bright young horse again.

Still, he'd never mentioned boarding a horse before. He was softening, the dear, and she appreciated that. "Oh, Thad," she said, deciding she had to be honest but not brutally so, "I can't think about marriage right now. Not with Steven in trouble, Uncle Bud in the hospital and the ranch burned down. I know I'm being unfair to put you off, but can't you wait until this thing with Steven's settled? It won't go on much longer. I'm sure he'll come to his senses and show up any day—any minute.''

She decided not to voice her doubts about her feelings for him ever deepening into love.

His expression was so hopeful and she feared she would hurt him badly if she uttered even one negative word. Besides, he'd made a big sacrifice for her. Maybe she ought to start thinking about doing the same thing for him. She kissed him. "You're a fine person, Thad. One of the finest I've ever known. To tell the truth, I'm not sure I'm good enough for you.''

He grinned softly. "You don't have to answer right now. We'll just leave it and one day soon you can just come up to me and say yes. How's that?''

She nodded, accepting the compromise. Every time she thought they had no future together, Thad did something so incredibly sweet. "Deal,'' she agreed, taking his hand in hers.

Once she'd sent Thad on his way with a quick hug and a wave, she found herself heading for Dusty's office, not sure why. Well, that wasn't quite true. She was sure now that she could never accept Thad's proposal as long as she reacted so strongly to Dusty. A little voice inside her was saying, *The man owns a company and a ranch, so maybe he's solid and steadfast underneath the fireworks and would love one woman forever.* She almost laughed aloud as an ironic thought struck her. If he could love one woman, why would he choose her? He certainly had no desire to be around her. He'd made that clear by avoiding her all week.

As she neared his office, she saw a faint glow of light from within, and her heart rate increased. Was he there?

She stood at the doorway and looked into the dimly lit room. Perhaps someone had accidentally left a lamp on ... Then she caught movement out of the corner of her eye.

Dusty was kneeling in the shadows in the far corner beside a low open cabinet. But what was he doing? Why hadn't he turned on another light? He almost looked as if he was stealing from his own house.

He picked up something from the floor that had been hidden from view. In the murky light, Anna could see that it was wooden. A carving of one, two—no, three running horses.

Three running horses?

That description matched Windchaser—the piece of art work Steven had stolen.

What was going on? For some reason, Dusty had been lying to her. He *was* holding the carving Steven had supposedly taken. Why was it here? What had really happened to her brother?

She must have gasped, because Dusty quickly turned toward her.

CHAPTER ELEVEN

"WHAT'S GOING ON?" she cried, as she stumbled forward to grasp the back of a chair. "Why do you have the carving you said Steven stole?"

"He *did* steal it," Dusty replied.

"Don't play games! How did it get back here?"

"It was sent by messenger eight days ago."

Her eyes widened. "*Eight days!* You let me worry for nothing for eight days?"

He straightened to his full height, his eyes never leaving hers. Placing the carving on the table beside him, he went to her. "Look, Anna, it's a long story. I hoped you wouldn't find out—"

"Where's my brother?" she demanded, cutting him off. "Is he okay?"

Dusty reached for her hand, but she jerked away. "Don't touch me, you... you liar. Now tell me—where's my brother?"

He shook his head and in distraction combed his fingers through his hair. "I don't know. I think he's okay. Look, trust me—"

"*Trust* you!" She gave a choked laugh. "I come in here to find you hiding your precious carving, which you've had back for over a week. Why should I trust you?" She took a breath. "But tell me one thing—if it's been here for a week, why are you just hiding it now?"

"It was delivered to my office. This was the first chance I've had to—"

"Oh, forget it! Why didn't you say anything? Was it because you needed a stable manager, and good old Frosty wasn't due for a few more days? That's it, isn't it! You let me worry myself sick about Steven going to jail, when all this time you only needed cheap help!" Her feeling of betrayal was strong, and she slapped him with the flat of her hand. The sound was loud in the quiet room, and her palm stung.

He touched the place she'd struck, but his grimace seemed to be caused by something else. "Damn." His voice was heavy with regret. "For your own good, Anna, don't push this." Turning, he walked out of the office, leaving her in a state of shock.

Tears stinging her eyes, she whimpered brokenly, "And . . . and I thought I was— Oh, my mother was right." She knew he couldn't possibly hear her, but she continued, "You're the kind of man who doesn't care about who you use as long as you get what you want!" She headed for the door. "You're not walking away from this!" she shouted, breaking into a run to catch up with him, though he was nowhere in sight. On a hunch, she dashed toward the stable. She found him in the yard throwing a saddle on Hazard. As he tightened the cinch, he spotted her. "Leave it be," he warned, then leapt into the saddle and kicked the stallion into a gallop.

Furious, Anna saddled Freckle and headed after him. They galloped through a moon-drenched field, the horse's hooves tearing at the sod as she rode recklessly into the woods.

Anna wasn't sure Dusty had even gone into the woods, but she had to find him and vent her rage. And then she'd...what? Make him explain how she could have fallen in love with a man who could do such a lousy selfish thing?

Suddenly she was sobbing and she could no longer see. She reined Freckle in, then swung down and threw herself against the rough bark of a pine. She had no idea where she was, and she didn't care. All she knew was that she'd almost allowed herself to ignore her mother's good advice—almost. Luckily Dusty had proved himself to be unworthy in time to save her from making a tragic mistake. "I *hate* you, Dusty Dare!" she wailed into the pine-scented night. "I hate you with all my heart and—"

"I don't blame you, sugar," a deep, hushed voice said. There was a gentle touch at her wrist, and then she was in his arms. "Dammit, Anna. Why did you have to follow me?"

"I have to know why you lied," she said fiercely, wishing her body wasn't thrilling to his touch.

"Hell and damnation, I can't." Some silly corner of her brain took note of the fact that he'd lost his hat and his hair was mussed. She hated herself for having the desire to reach up and savor the feel of it. "Anna—" her name was a plea as he drew her close "—I know you hate me, but before you leave, I want to tell you something."

Dizzy with feelings of longing and loathing, she pushed against his chest. "I don't want to hear—"

"I love you," he whispered, his voice a hoarse rasp. The husky vow washed over her, making her ache, and she could only stare, speechless as he went on, "I guess I've been too busy fighting or working to get very involved with any woman. Hell," he conceded, "Brett did enough of that for both of us, but—" He stopped.

Anna pulled away slightly to better see his face. His expression was one of complete sincerity. She swallowed hard at the sight. "But what?" she asked weakly, feeling herself helplessly drawn by the power of his hypnotic eyes.

"But my lack of involvement hasn't been because I can't love a woman with all my heart. I just hadn't found her." He surveyed her caressingly. "When I met you nothing else seemed to matter—not that your brother was a thief or that you hated my guts or—" his lips twisted bitterly "—or even that you had that greenhorn boyfriend—fiancé, now, I suppose." His voice roughened. "It made me mad to love a woman I shouldn't love, couldn't have, and I guess I took my anger out on you. I'm sorry."

She was trembling, his nearness affecting her even after he'd lied to her. But he was saying he loved her! She felt such pain in her heart she feared she was being ripped in two. How could he say that? She couldn't ever trust him, not after he'd used her.

With a strangled cry, she shoved him away, trying to escape. When she was unsuccessful, she lifted both fists in thwarted anger. She was aware that he tensed his body in preparation for her attack. Yet he didn't let her go. He took her pummeling without flinching.

Defeat flooding through her, she pounded harder against his chest, crying brokenly, "You love me?" She laughed, hearing the hysteria there. "You couldn't really love me and let me worry myself sick! Why..." Her voice broke and she swallowed in an effort to control it. "Why did you do it?"

"I— Dammit, I *can't* tell you."

She went still. He had no reason. No excuse. She pushed against his chest. "Then, let me *go!*"

Frustration crossed his features, but he did as she'd insisted, releasing her so suddenly she stumbled backward. Awkwardly regaining her balance, she looked at him and saw bitterness on his face, but somehow she realized it wasn't directed at her. And beyond that, she thought she could see pain and remorse. She was touched, but she still refused to soften.

Wanting only to escape, she floundered backward, bumping into Freckle. She swung into the saddle and paused for one last look at him—a handsome man standing in the moonlight. He would be in her heart for a very long time. "I won't forget this, Mr. Dare. Just you remember—paybacks are hell!"

She rode back to the house and stabled Freckle, then jumped into her truck and sped away. She'd gone several miles before she realized how stupidly she was acting. Where did she think she was going? She had no place to go. Her family home was a pile of ashes, her uncle was in the hospital, and her brother—who *knew* where he was?

She slowed and pulled over to the gravel shoulder of the road. She considered her pitifully few options, and after a few moments, she pulled the truck back onto the road and headed toward Tulsa. Thad would put her up—and he'd probably even give her a very low rate. She licked her lips nervously. She'd made up her mind. Dusty's cruel deceit had put everything in perspective. Now that she'd been burned by the fireworks, she harbored no more silly fantasies about him. She was officially Thad's fiancée, although he didn't know it yet.

She'd told Thad she'd give him her answer after Steven's situation was settled. And all of a sudden it was. Not the way she would have liked perhaps. But now she could get on with her life.

After the twenty-minute drive, Anna parked in Elite's garage. As she got off the garage elevator and crossed the plush jade carpeting to the marble-and-brass front desk, she thought about how she must look. For that matter, her beat-up truck didn't bear any resemblance to the luxury cars parked all around it. But months ago Thad had given her an executive parking pass, so the security guard hadn't asked any questions.

The green-vested night clerk looked up from his book and smiled. "May I help you, miss?" he asked, laying aside his book and giving her his undivided attention.

"Yes," she said. "I was hoping to speak to Mr. Kelly, the manager?"

The clerk's smile faltered. "I'm afraid he's unavailable at this time."

She nodded tiredly. "I understand. May I use a house phone, please? I'm a friend of his."

The clerk nodded, indicating a bank of golden phones on a green marble table at one end of the reception area.

She dialed Thad's room. The phone rang five, six, seven times. She was just about to hang up when it was answered. "Yeah? Um, yes?"

"Thad..." Anna whispered, surprised that her voice was failing her.

There was a pause, then, "Anna? Is that you?" He sounded more alert. "Something wrong? It isn't your uncle, is it?"

"No, no," she said, "Thad, I...I need a room for the night. I've left the ranch."

"A room? We're full up. Our new 'Spend a Romantic Evening with Elite' advertising campaign's really been working. And the floor we're refurbishing doesn't have any furniture in place." He paused, and Anna could tell he was trying to come up with an idea. "Uh, now don't take this wrong, but you can stay in my suite. I've got that pullout couch in the living room."

Anna sighed. "Oh, I don't know. You're wonderful to offer, but—"

"Look, sweetie, you know how I feel about you. But if you're not ready for anything else, I'll honor that. Please, use the couch."

She smiled, grateful that there was at least one person she could count on. "Thanks, Thad. I don't have any bags. I'm afraid I left in a hurry."

"What did that guy do?" he demanded, suddenly suspicious. "Did he try something?"

"It wasn't like that." A bleakness washed over her. "Look, can I come on up?"

"Uh...sure." He paused, then chuckled. "I guess I'm still woozy. When I take my sinus medicine, I sleep like the dead, and it takes me a while to get my brain working. I'll throw on a robe and meet you at the elevator." He hung up so fast she didn't have time to tell him not to bother.

When the elevator arrived at the tenth floor, Thad was hustling down the hall, smoothing his flyaway hair as he came. He had on red-and-white-striped pajamas and a white seersucker robe that was flapping behind him.

This vulnerability was something she'd rarely seen. Thad was competent in his job and extremely good-natured, with a streak of insecurity he tried desperately to hide. At this minute, he looked so dear she felt a new tenderness build in her heart. Thad Kelly would never lie to her, never betray her trust. She decided that even if they never shared a burning passion, she could love him for his trustworthiness alone.

"Hi," she said, smiling softly as he rushed to take her in his arms.

"Hi, yourself." He kissed her, then stepped back to look at her. "So tell me. Why did you leave the ranch in the middle of the night?"

She shrugged, taking his arm. "We can talk about it tomorrow. You need to get your rest."

"Whatever you want, sweetie." When they reached his door, he gave her a hopeful grin. "Do you have anything in particular you want to say to me?"

She was puzzled. "What do you mean?"

"If you don't know, I guess I'll keep my mouth shut."

He opened the paneled door and let her precede him into his apartment. She'd been in the suite many times. It smelled of rosy potpourri and had the feel of an English country house. But Anna thought it was a bit overfurnished with the heavy antiques Thad had inherited from his grandmother.

One of the living-room walls was covered with bookshelves filled with leather-bound volumes about the Civil War, a passion of Thad's. He could talk for hours on the subject—and often did. Along the top of the shelves, Thad's collection of one-of-a-kind chess pieces—his other abiding passion—was displayed. She smiled mockingly, wondering where she'd fit into things—abiding passion-wise.

Suddenly she realized what Thad had wanted to know. He'd been hoping she was there to accept his marriage proposal. Her heart sank, and she began to twist her braid nervously as he showed her where the linens were kept, got her a T-shirt to sleep in and helped her unfold the bed. How could she have forgotten? He'd only proposed an hour and a half ago!

Thad gave her a peck on the cheek and headed to his bedroom and his vaporizer, leaving her to her privacy. Watching him go, seersucker fluttering in his wake, she felt a rush of shame at her lack of sensitivity. Sighing, she plopped down on the thin creaky mattress and began to unbutton her blouse. She supposed there'd been no real harm done. She *was* going to say yes, wasn't she?

THE NIGHT WIND whistled through the trees, making the branches above Dusty's head bob and clatter together like brittle bones. He lifted his head from his hand and peered at his watch. The luminous dial glowed in the faint moonlight. Four-ten in the morning. Exhaling heavily, he leaned wearily against the rough tree trunk. Anna had driven away four hours ago. Even this far from the house, he'd heard her truck's echoing backfire. Thinking she needed the time to cool off, he'd resisted the urge to go after her. But he thought she'd have come back by now.

The first hour after she'd gone, he'd cursed himself for not making sure the office door was closed when he'd been hiding that carving. Downright jackass stupid of him! But how was he to know she'd show up at that time of night?

The second hour after she'd gone, he'd begun to worry. That truck of hers was a piece of junk and ready to fall apart. What if it had broken down, or she'd had an accident? What if she was lying in some muddy ditch? He forced himself to be calm. No, it was more likely she'd gone to a friend's. Or maybe the hospital where her uncle was.

He vaulted to his feet, unable to stand the lack of action one moment longer. He had to know if she was all right. Mounting Hazard, he headed for the stable at a full gallop. Once there he hurriedly took care of Hazard, then threw open the door to Anna's office and grabbed the phone book out of her desk's bottom drawer. Finding the hospital's number and dialing, he was connected to the night desk on her uncle's floor, but Anna wasn't there.

With a white-knuckled grip on the receiver, he made a decision he hadn't even wanted to think about. He'd call Thad Kelly. Murderous resentment coursing through his veins, he flipped to the *K*'s in the phone book and scanned the page for Thad's number. Ah, there it was.

Dusty dialed. It was too soon to call the police, and as Anna's fiancé, Thad had a right to know. Of course, there was always the chance that she was with him. As the phone began to ring, Dusty swallowed the bile that rose in his throat at the thought.

One ring, two—"Hello?" came a drowsy female voice.

Dusty's body shuddered with a combination of fierce relief and blinding loss. She was okay, but she was with another man. He clenched his teeth to keep from howling in outrage. The woman he loved, loved someone else.

"Hello?" came the soft sleepy voice again. "Is anyone there?"

Dusty's gut twisted as he pictured her. Long tawny hair splayed across the pillow—another man's pillow. Without a word, he lowered the receiver into its cradle. "Goodbye, Anna," he murmured.

Rising, he paced to the glass-paned door that led outside. Violence building inside him, he drew back a fist, wanting to smash every damned thing in the world.

He stopped himself. Ramming flesh and bone through glass would resolve nothing. With a curse, he placed his hands on the door frame and stared up at the night sky.

A skinny slice of moon hung low, but now the scudding clouds were gone and stars winked in the blackness. To him the crescent moon looked like a leering Cheshire cat. Probably the same cat-ate-the-canary grin Thad Kelly was wearing right now.

Worn-out from days of worry and nights without sleep, Dusty rested his forehead against the cool glass and closed his eyes. Unfortunately the only vision he managed to shut out was the smirking moon. Anna, with her damned beautiful hair and her damned beautiful eyes, was still there.

He swore. "Sugar, you really know how to hurt a guy."

ANNA FUMBLED with the receiver, confused. "Hello?" she said again, rising on an elbow, trying to clear the cobwebs of sleep from her head. It had taken her a long time, but she'd eventually fallen into a deep sleep, and she was having trouble waking up. Something cold touched her lips, and she frowned in bewilderment, then realized what was wrong. She wasn't at home, or even at the ranch. This was Thad's place, and the phone she'd grabbed was a fancy brass-and-porcelain thing that sat on the table beside the pull-out couch.

The other party had hung up, and the dial tone was humming in her ear. More than anything she wanted it to have been Dusty calling to tell her the truth. She shook her head. How stupid. Dusty didn't know she was here. Besides, it was the middle of the night; he'd be in bed now. And, after what she'd said, why would he care if she were alive or dead?

As she started to replace the receiver, she heard another voice. "Uh, he-hello?"

It was Thad, belatedly answering the phone. "Hi, Thad," she said over the dial tone.

"Huh? Who's this?"

"It's Anna, Thad. It's—"

"Anna?" he asked, sounding punchy, his sinus medication obviously affecting him. "Why are you calling? Where are you?"

"I'm still in the living room," she explained. "The phone rang and I answered it. Nobody said anything." Trying to ease her own tension, she kidded, "Must have been one of your other girlfriends. Do you have a rule—if a woman answers, hang up?"

He laughed, sounding more awake. "Yeah, sure. I'm a regular Don Juan."

She smiled halfheartedly, picturing his striped pajamas. He looked more like a candy cane than a great lover. Then she made a sudden decision. There was no point in putting him off any longer. Thad was such a good guy, and he loved her so much, there was no reason not tell him what he wanted to hear. "Well, Mr. Juan..." The words caught in her throat, and she cleared it nervously. "I thought you'd like to know," she whispered, "my answer's yes."

There was a long pause and all Anna could hear was the drone of the dial tone.

"Are you kidding?" he asked at last, sounding breathless and wide awake.

"I'm serious, Thad. My answer is yes."

"Well, heck, this calls for a kiss, don't you think?"

She flushed, not having thought that far ahead. "I guess... but, let's wait till morning. I mean, I'm not decent. Okay?"

Anna had a feeling Thad wanted to object, but all he said was, "Well, okay. And Anna? I hope you know you've made me a happy man."

She smiled, despite the fact that she didn't feel like a particularly happy woman. "Th-thank you. Uh, good night... darling." Hanging up, she lay back on her pillow to stare at the darkened ceiling.

"This is for the best," she murmured. She was suddenly very, very weary.

"QUIT TREATING ME like a bronc with a busted leg," Uncle Bud grumbled as Anna brought him his breakfast on a tray. For the past two weeks he'd been recuperating on the second floor of the Elite Hotel, in a room that was connected to hers. Uncle Bud didn't like being cooped up, but since they hadn't had fire insurance, there was no telling when they'd get their ranch house rebuilt.

Thad had been wonderful about accommodations, arranging for free rooms on the floor that was being renovated. He'd had some furniture brought in, mismatched and scarred, but serviceable. The green shag carpet and gold-and-green curtains with a swirling wave design were at least twenty years old. But Anna didn't care.

She slid the breakfast tray onto the rickety table that sat before the window. Her uncle was sitting next to it on a straight back chair. The sagging bed was on his other side. "Now, Uncle Bud, you know the doctor said you couldn't get back on a horse for a while. That bout with pneumonia left you pretty run-down. So relax and enjoy the sunshine."

He muttered under his breath and loudly snapped open the paper she'd brought. Twisting around on the chair, he placed it on the bed. Anna grimaced when he turned a few pages and came to the society section. Her engagement picture stuck out like a sore thumb.

"Holy Cow." He smoothed the page lovingly. "You look purtier than a speckled calf in a field of daisies, Punkin." He glanced up at her, his face creased in a grin. "Never saw me sech a sight since your ma married that wild scalawag—" He stopped himself.

Anna's breath caught painfully. They both knew he'd been about to say "Abe." Uncle Bud cleared his throat. "Well, anywho, you're the spittin' image of your purty ma."

"Thanks, Uncle Bud," she said, leaning down to kiss his forehead. "Now eat your breakfast before it gets cold."

"Who cares if that baby grub gets cold? Ain't enough there to put a speck o' gristle on these old bones."

"The doctor said with your blood pressure, you need to watch your salt and cholesterol," Anna cajoled, lifting the metal cover from his breakfast of oatmeal, dry wheat toast, orange juice and decaffeinated coffee.

"That quack don't know no more about my innards than a hog knows about a ruffled dress. That dratted stuff keeps me emptier'n a gutted steer."

She shook her head at him. "You've just got cabin fever. That's your problem."

He squinted up at her. "Yeah? Well, I ain't seen you singing no praises to the city lights. You been lookin' awful poorly for a gal about to get hitched." He inclined his head, his features scrunching in worried compassion. "You got somethin' gnawin' at you, Punkin?"

She shook her head. She hadn't brought up Dusty's name since she'd left the ranch and didn't want to talk about him. It was bad enough that he was never really far from her thoughts. "I'm fine," she said with a counterfeit grin that didn't last long. "I guess I'm just suffering from cabin fever, too."

He grunted, eyeing her speculatively. "You goin' back out to Euby Hobbs's place to work with their cuttin' stock today?"

She managed a genuine grin. "Sure. We've got to earn the money to rebuild our place, don't we?"

"Shoot, 'cept for them goats at Mr. Dare's house, Hobbs is boardin' all our livestock. We're doing nothin' but comin' out even. Where's the money gonna come from for the house?"

Anna took hold of her braid and started to flip the end back and forth. "Don't worry, Uncle Bud. We'll get you that house."

He ran a bony hand through his snowy curls and coughed. "With me out there trainin', too, we'd earn the money twice as fast."

She smiled encouragingly. "When you can walk all the way across this room without the cane, then we'll see."

Clearly irritated, he glared at his breakfast, then shakily poured himself a cup of coffee. "You're a good niece, Punkin," he said, taking a sip. "More'n I can say for your no 'count brother. Where do you figure he's been holdin' up?"

She lost her smile and turned away. "I wish I knew." Wanting to change the subject, she said as lightheartedly as she could, "Tell you what—tomorrow we'll pack a picnic, and you can sit under a tree while I work the horses. That'll give you the chance to yell at me and tell me what I'm doing wrong. What do you say?"

He dropped the spoonful of oatmeal he'd had halfway to his lips and it fell back in the bowl with a loud clank. "Yahoo!"

She grinned, despite her nagging worries. Where was the money going to come from to rebuild their home? Her uncle would die if he had to stay cooped up here much longer. And to be perfectly honest, Anna was afraid she would, too.

Her gaze went to her picture, smiling up from the newspaper as if she didn't have a care in the world. If only that were true. For she'd grown to hate this hotel and its closed-in, airless world. The past two weeks had slid by in a dreary daze. She'd gone through the preparations for the wedding like a zombie, putting all doubts about what she was doing from her mind. She knew she should be walking on air. But deep in her heart she also knew there was something missing from her relationship with Thad. Something essential.

Glancing at her left hand, she listlessly twisted the diamond solitaire that glittered there, but felt no happiness at what it represented. And she knew why. She hadn't seen or heard from Dusty since she'd left the ranch—not that she was surprised. Still, her thoughts constantly strayed to him. She had a feeling Thad could tell things weren't right between them, and she blamed herself for that.

Thad was as attentive as ever. He didn't deserve half a wife. But she'd told him yes. The engagement had been officially announced and the invitations were at the printers. She twisted the ring again. What was she going to do?

"You gonna get that, Punkin?" asked her uncle, drawing her from her worries.

She jerked around, frowning in confusion. Then she heard it. The phone was ringing. With a lethargic heaviness in her limbs, she moved to the night table on the other side of the bed and lifted the receiver. "Hello?"

"Annie, kid? Is that you?"

Anna lowered herself shakily to the mattress. "Steven..." she whispered, hardly daring to believe her ears.

CHAPTER TWELVE

"YEAH, IT'S ME, your long-lost brother," Steven said with a tense chuckle. "Wanted to sorta fill you and Uncle Bud in on what I'm up to these days."

Anna clutched the phone for dear life. "It's about time. Where in heaven's name are you? Where've you been? Uncle Bud and I have been worried sick!"

There was such a lengthy pause on the line Anna feared her brother might have hung up. "Steven? Are you there?"

"Uh, yeah, I'm here. I just don't understand why you don't know." He paused again and cleared his throat. "Look, I'm in the hotel lobby. Maybe I could come up?"

Anna gasped. "Of course! Come right up."

"Thanks, kid," he said, then hung up.

Anna ran to the elevator and threw herself into his arms when the doors opened. Grabbing his hand, she tugged him along. "Come on. Uncle Bud's a little weak, but he's crazy to see you."

Once in Bud's room, Steven sat hunched on the other chair, his elbows on his knees. Anna noticed that he was dressed well. His shirt was pressed, his jeans were new and his boots shined. He held his straw hat between his knees, uneasily fingering the curled brim. He didn't make eye contact, just stared at the floor. "I'm sorry I didn't call," he muttered. "But I thought you knew where I was."

"Now, how would we know that, boy?" Bud asked, hobbling over to lower himself on the bed near Steven's chair. He reached out and squeezed his nephew's shoulder.

Steven glanced up, his brows knit in consternation. Anna's heart went out to him. He looked ten pounds thinner. Though he was a good-looking blond with bedroom-blue eyes and a muscular stature that girls admired, he seemed fragile, vulnerable. "I can't figure it," he said morosely. "Didn't Dusty tell you?"

"Tell us what?" Anna whispered, every bit as bewildered as Steven sounded. "I haven't seen him for two weeks, not since I found out he had the carving back. He refused to tell me anything about that, so I left."

"Oh, er, right," Steven mumbled guiltily. His gaze drifted back to the floor. "That was before."

"Before? Before what?" Anna asked, joining her uncle on the edge of the bed. "Steven, you're not making any sense."

"I'm sorry, kid. Maybe I'd better start at the beginning."

"Maybe you better, boy," Bud agreed. "You put your sister and me through a lot o' worry."

Steven grimaced. "Well, first of all, you know I stole the carving and ran off to try to sell it."

"Yes, we know all about that," Anna murmured.

"Okay. When I finally got the word Dusty wouldn't press charges if I returned the carving, I'd already found out no one would take a chance on buying it—just like you told me. So it wasn't doing me any good. I figured, if I sent it back, it'd save our ranch and me some jail time. But I begged Dusty not to tell you, 'cause the guys who were after me had threatened to kill me, and I didn't want you to worry about that, too."

"Threatened to—" Anna's voice caught "—kill you?"

"Yeah." He ran a fist across his nose. "When you owe these guys fifty thousand dollars, they get riled if you run out on 'em. Real riled. Anyway, I wrote a note to Dusty and stuck it in the box with the carving, begging him not to tell you about everything."

"Oh, Steven!" Anna cried, feeling the blood drain from her face.

"See, Anna, I knew you'd get hysterical. That's why I begged Dusty not to say anything till I got the money. I figured if it got around that I didn't have the carving anymore, they'd know I didn't have a way to pay them their money, and I'd be a dead man."

She shook her head. "So, that's why he wouldn't tell me."

"Huh?" Steven looked confused.

Tears welled in her eyes as she recalled the awful names she'd called Dusty. Forcing her mind back to the present, she said, "S-so, what's happening, Steven? What about the . . . the guys you owe money to?"

He slouched back in his chair, looking weary. "See—after the ranch burned, Dusty figured it might be arson. You know, that they were trying to scare me into paying. So he asked the cops to check it out. When they told him there was evidence the fire was deliberately set, he knew I was telling the truth. So Dusty hired a private detective to find the guys who were looking for me."

"Why?" Anna asked, running her hand over her eyes. She was strangely dizzy. There was just too much information for her to take in.

"I found out later that Dusty bought my marker."

"I don't understand. What does that mean?"

Uncle Bud patted her knee. "It means Mr. Dare paid the fifty thousand, and now Steve owes it to him. That right, boy?"

Steven nodded, and Anna whispered incredulously. "Steven owes Dusty?"

"Yeah," Steven admitted. "Anyway, Dusty's PI found me hiding out in Texas. He told me the jerks were off my back and that Dusty bought my debt. All I had to do was get myself into Gamblers Anonymous, get a job and start paying him back outa my salary. I'm working outside Dallas at the Silver Q. Seems their trainer just quit." He shrugged. "Dusty called 'em ten days ago to tell 'em I was in town. Told 'em that I was in GA, but that I was a good worker. 'Course I have to stay in GA, or the job's history. I've been working there a week, and they like me fine. I've been going to GA meetings most evenings, and I'm feeling pretty good about everything." He allowed himself a small grin. "Just wanted to come up and say I'm sorry in person." He stood, still fidgeting with his hat.

Anna jumped up to hug him, unable to hold back her tears of happiness. "Oh, Steven, I'm so relieved. The Silver Q's top notch. You'll do fine."

He put his arms around her and kissed her cheek. "I'm gonna work hard, and I owe one heck of a lot to Dusty—getting my hide outa trouble the way he did." When Anna released him, he shook his head ruefully. "It's my fault about the ranch, too, but I'll pay you back for that someday.... How are you two making out?"

"We'll be fine," Bud said, squeezing his nephew's hand. "We all will."

They shared a smile. In the quiet moment, a thought struck Anna. "How'd you find out where we were?"

"Dusty told me you were staying here."

She was confused. "How did he know?"

Steven laughed. "Seems like that guy knows everything. Look, kid—" his features went serious "—I owe Dusty a ton of money. But as soon as I can, I'll start sending some up to help you both."

Anna wiped a tear from her cheek. "You know, Steven, you seem . . . different. I really think you're telling me the truth."

"I'm being as straight as a shotgun barrel, kid." He sniffed, and Anna was startled to see tears glimmering in his eyes. "I'd better go. Gotta get back to Dallas. They only gave me the one day off."

"Okay." She hugged him tightly. "I love you."

And then he was gone. She went to sit beside her uncle and took his hand. Neither of them spoke.

"Why, Punkin," her uncle said finally, lifting his gnarled old hand to stroke her hair, "you're cryin'."

"Oh, Uncle Bud," she moaned, "I've been so wrong about Dusty. Even that day when he dropped me off at the hospital and didn't come in, I though he was cold-hearted. Now I know he was going to talk to the police about the fire."

Uncle Bud studied her face. "Maybe I shouldn't stick my big nose into your life, but I been feeling for some time that you got some business with that man you need to work out."

BY THE TIME Anna returned to the hotel after training Euby's horses, she'd had all day to think about what Steven had told her and what her uncle had said. She finally had to face the fact that she'd been in love with Dusty from the first minute she'd set eyes on him.

But she was sure Dusty didn't want her in his life. He'd had nothing to do with her since she'd left his ranch. Unfortunately that fact didn't make her love him any less.

This afternoon she'd tried to figure out a way to stop. But she'd failed. Although her mother's advice had been wise and Thad was very kind, she couldn't help the way she felt. She knew there was only one fair thing to do. She had to break the news to Thad that she couldn't marry him, and she had to do it soon. He deserved a wife who would love him completely.

She approached Thad's suite feeling fairly calm, considering what she was about to do. Twisting her engagement ring around and around, she finally tugged it off. Making a fist around it, she knocked on Thad's door. He'd said he'd be going over some redecorating estimates tonight, but she had to interrupt. This was too important to put off.

When he opened the door he was smiling, saying, "You're early with dinner. Just set it—" His grin faded. "Anna! I wasn't expecting you."

"I know, Thad, it's just that I have to tell you something that can't wait."

"Oh." He frowned. "Sure. What is it?"

Misgivings skittered along her spine. Something wasn't right. He was holding a glass half full of a clear liquid and decorated with a twist of lemon. He wasn't inviting her inside, and he was wearing his new houndstooth-check sport jacket. Awfully dressy attire for going over estimates. "May I come in?" she asked. "This is rather private."

He swallowed and nervously glanced over his shoulder. "Look, Anna," he said, obviously uncomfortable, "this is awkward. But I've been meaning to talk to you, too. About us."

Curious, Anna peered around him and saw a woman with short red hair sitting at his chess table, sipping from a wineglass. Anna's gaze veered back to Thad. "Isn't that the woman from the hospital?"

He grimaced, as though caught with his hand in the cookie jar. "Um, yes, it is. See—" he exhaled long and loudly, as if searching for words "—I don't know how to say this, Anna, but things haven't been, you know, clicking with you and me, and, well, I ran into Lydia last week at the Jim Dandy's Drug Emporium. We were both refilling our allergy prescriptions, so we got to talking about the unbelievable mold-spore count this month and—" He stopped, running a finger under his shirt collar. "Anyway, I found out she loves chess, and would you believe, Lydia and I are allergic to exactly the same stuff? It's eerie how much we have in common...."

Anna stared at him perplexed, then the irony of the situation struck her. "Why, Thad Kelly," she breathed, incredulous, "you're dumping me, aren't you."

He winced. "Don't say it like that. You and I both know something's missing between us. You've changed—I can't put my finger on what it is exactly." He reached out and squeezed her arm. "You've been trying not to show it, and I love you for that, but let's face it, you're not happy when you're with me, and you should be—that is, if you really loved me." He lowered his voice to barely a whisper. "You know I'll always love you, but..."

"I understand," she cut in softly. Then, with a rueful smile she uncurled her fingers to display the ring. "Maybe you ought to take this back. I have a feeling you'll find a better use for it."

His features closed in a bewildered frown. But after a few seconds, he smiled. "You're not angry?"

She shook her head, dropping the ring into his breast pocket. "Not a bit. Good luck to you and Lydia—and congratulations on your matching mold-spore thing."

He chuckled self-consciously. "You're a great girl, Anna. And the rooms downstairs are yours as long as you and your uncle need them." He kissed her cheek. "Friends?"

She hugged him. "Always, Thad."

When he'd reentered his suite and closed the door, she sagged against the wall feeling both great relief and new terror. "You know what you have to do now," she muttered to herself, not sure she had the courage.

ANNA FEARED a trip to Bent River Ranch was a fool's errand, but she forced herself to climb into her truck and head there.

Darn it! Even though she was alarmed about facing Dusty, she was indebted to him for everything he'd done for Steven, and she knew she'd never rest until she'd apologized. So she'd kissed her uncle good-night, told him she'd see him in the morning and left to make her groveling amends.

She was admitted to the house by a startled, yet clearly pleased Max, and ushered into a parlor down a hall in the wing opposite from Dusty's office. She'd never been in this room before. The walls were mustard yellow, the floor terra-cotta. The furnishings were Western in design and an interesting Spanish grandfather clock dominated the far wall. Brown Spanish pottery adorned the tile mantel over the fireplace and sat in decorative disorder on a long low set of bookshelves.

She wandered around for a few minutes, then perched on the brown leather couch. After five more minutes, footfalls in the hallway made her stiffen. Someone was approaching. A man. She frowned; it didn't sound like Dusty. There was an easiness to this tread that she'd never heard in his.

She stared fearfully at the closed door. What if Dusty had refused to see her? She hadn't thought of that. The door swung wide and a stranger entered. He was very like Dusty in coloring, but, although there were other similarities, somehow he was not as impressive as Dusty.

He smiled politely. "So, you're Miss Andrews? I'm Brett Dare, Dusty's big brother."

Of course. Back from his honeymoon. "Nice to meet you, Mr. Dare." She came abruptly to her feet. "I . . . I was hoping to see Mr., er, Dusty. I'm sorry if there was some confusion."

He laughed. It was a deep bold sound so like Dusty's it made her tingle. "No confusion. Dusty's out of town. Let's see, he's either in Texas buying a company, or performing in the Trail of Tears pageant in Tahlequah." He shrugged carelessly and ambled over to hold out a hand. "I understand you took up the slack around here during our emergency last month, and I want to thank you."

She accepted his hand, preparing to leave. "It was the least I could do. . ." The sentence trailed away, her cheeks going hot at the reminder of Steven's theft. "I'm sorry I bothered you so late. I wasn't really thinking. You see, I saw Steven today for the first time since—uh, anyway, he told me everything Dusty did for him, and, well, then Thad and I broke off our engagement. I don't know, I just wanted..." She swallowed, aware that she was prattling on, but wasn't able to stop. "I just wanted to say I need to see Dusty in person to apologize for the things I said before I left. I wouldn't blame him if he doesn't want to see me, but... Oh, maybe I'd just better go."

"I tell you what," Brett said, checking his watch. "Why not stay here for the night and have brunch with me and Patty and Nicole tomorrow." His grin had broadened inexplicably. "I hear we have you to thank for her new hobby."

"Me?" She was embarrassed by running off at the mouth the way she had and was grateful for a change of subject. "What hobby?"

"Tuba lessons. How could you forget?"

He made a wry face which Anna found so charming she actually smiled back. "How is Nicole?"

"The little squirt's going steady with another tuba player from her music class, so she's as blissful as any fifteen-year-old can be." He crossed his arms and sighed in mock exasperation. "The young stud comes over here, and the two of them play their tubas for the goats. They must be getting better. The goats hardly ever faint anymore."

She grinned in spite of her anxiety. "That reminds me. I appreciate your keeping them for us. Please bill us for—"

"Nonsense," he interrupted. "Nicole wouldn't part with them. We owe you for renting them to us." Surprising her, he took her by the arm. "Say, Miss Andrews—"

"Call me Anna, please."

"Okay, then, Anna. I know Nicole would love to see you, and I want you to meet Patty. Stay over and have breakfast. Besides, I think Dusty'll be getting back fairly early. You could say your piece to him without making another trip out here. Kill three or four birds with one stone. And I saved the best for last." He lifted a teasing brow. "Nicole might be convinced to play her tuba for you. Or she might be convinced not to, if you bribe her."

Anna's shy grin returned. When the Dare brothers put on the charm, they were hard to resist. She gave a start when the grandfather clock loudly started to chime midnight. Raising her voice over the din, she said, "I had no idea it was this late. I shouldn't have bothered you without calling first."

"No problem," he protested, dropping his hand to her wrist. "I'm a night person, anyway. And no offense, but I heard that truck of yours coming half a mile away. It would be negligent of me to send you back out at this hour when the chances that you'll break down on some lonely country road are bigger than the national debt. I insist you wait until daylight before heading back. You can use Dusty's room.''

Anna stumbled to a stop. "But I—"

He grinned. "It's like this. Patty's redecorating, and I just remembered that Dusty's is the only spare room in the place that doesn't reek of paint. I wouldn't want to asphyxiate you. Wouldn't be neighborly. My brother's not here, so what's the problem?''

She felt odd being led to Dusty's bedroom, but she supposed it was silly of her. She'd be up and eating breakfast before he got home. Besides, Brett seemed determined to have his way.

She only hoped she'd be able to sleep in a room with Dusty's scent everywhere, reminding her of him. In spite of herself, she inhaled deeply. His black straw Stetson was sitting on a wheat-colored, hand-woven bedspread. A pair of black boots lolled beside a twig rocking chair that was draped by a Navaho blanket with geometric designs in cream, black and rust.

The place had such a comfortable, lived-in feel she couldn't shake the notion that Dusty might walk in at any second, slide on those boots, plant his hat on his head and grin in that sexy way he had—that was, until he recognized her and threw her out on her backside. The unhappy thought made her stomach twist, and she couldn't quite stifle a groan. Looking apprehensively in Brett's direction, she prayed he hadn't heard her, but his expression revealed nothing.

After Brett left, she walked around the room. On a chest of drawers she spied a bronze eagle, its wings stretched wide in flight, as though it was soaring through the sky in unchallenged sovereignty. Drawn by its spirit and strength, she trailed her fingers along the cool metal. The intense stare inherent vitality and supple beauty of the wild creature re minded her of Dusty. Her heart filled with longing. "Oh, Dusty, why must I love you so?"

ANNA WAS HAVING a terrifyingly real nightmare. She was being swept into the vortex of a tornado; its roaring winds were deafening, and the pain of being banged around in the deadly maelstrom made her flinch and moan. The breath went out of her as something hard hit her stomach, and she whimpered, her eyes coming open in panic.

It was dark, too dark, but she was sure she was awake. Still, she felt a gouging pain in her stomach and heard the bellowing wind. Except...

Except the wind was cursing.

She gasped for air, realizing she'd been tossed over a broad shoulder, bedclothes and all, and was being hauled off to some unknown destination.

An excruciating few seconds ticked by when the pain in her stomach came in frequent bouncy blows. She had the feeling she was moving rapidly downward, but the bedspread draped over her head made it difficult to be sure.

Frightened, she pounded on the kidnapper's back and cried out, "Let me—oof—down! Let—oof—go of me!" Her breathy demands sounded muffled even in her own ears. She wasn't certain her captor could hear her at all.

Without warning, she was swept through the air, and then her bare feet came in contact with a cool wooden floor. Off balance she swatted at the sheets until her head was free. Shaking her tangled hair from her face, she spat out, "What's going on!" She froze as she saw who'd dragged her from her bed and dropped her in the entry hall.

"Dusty?" she squeaked, suddenly aware of her state of undress, having worn only her flimsy camisole and panties to bed. Dismayed, she grasped the spread about her. "I...I..." but nothing coherent would come out.

He was standing there, looking every bit as shocked as she was. Clad in jeans and a beige cotton shirt open halfway down his chest, it was obvious he'd just begun to undress before noticing that someone was in his bed.

Doubt and confusion in his eyes, he demanded, "What the hell were you doing in my room?"

"Little brother, if that's your idea of seduction, no wonder you've never married," called a male voice from the landing above. They both looked up at Brett. He was beaming down at them, wearing nothing but a pair of jeans. "Afraid the little goat lady's presence in your bed was my doing. You've been off your feed lately, so I thought I'd try a little experiment. Now I think I'll just mosey on back to bed. I've done my part."

"Your part?" Dusty snarled. "What the hell does that mean?"

Brett's laughter echoed back, but he said nothing.

Dusty turned to face Anna. "What the hell's going on?"

She hiked up the bedspread, feeling exposed and humiliated. With her chin jutting defensively, she retorted weakly, "He told me you wouldn't be back tonight. Said he wanted me to meet Patty and see Nicole." She bit her lip. Brett had done this on purpose, and she couldn't imagine why he'd decided to be so cruel. What had she ever done to him?

In the tense quiet, Dusty's angry frown turned wary. "Brett knew I'd be driving back from Tahlequah tonight."

She stiffened her spine, deciding to stand there and take whatever he dished out. "Maybe so. But I didn't! I know you dislike me, but I can't see why your brother would want to humiliate me. You Dare men are heavily into paybacks, aren't you? And to think I came out here to ask you to forgive me."

"Forgive you? For what?"

"For all the nasty things I said when I left," she admitted tightly. "Steven . . . Steven came to see me this morning, er, yesterday morning—whatever." She shook her head glumly. "Anyway, I wanted to say I'm sorry, okay? I was vicious to you, and now that I know why you couldn't tell me everything, I want to apologize." Distractedly she pushed her disheveled mass of hair away from her face.

A muscle began to throb in his jaw. "You have nothing to apologize for."

"Tell him about your engagement," commanded Brett from the landing.

They both turned to stare at Brett. He shrugged and grinned. "Do I have to do everything? Dammit, Dusty, she's not engaged to that greenhorn 'cowboy' anymore." He winked at Anna. "You tell him, Anna. I need my beauty sleep." With that he walked out of sight. But this time they heard a door close in the distance and knew they were alone.

Anna glanced at Dusty. His face was closed, cautious. "Is that true?"

She nodded, but stiffly, embarrassed by Brett's actions. "That's not why I came, though," she blurted in self-defense, "I wanted you to forgive me. I wanted to thank you for helping Steven." She squeezed her eyes shut, feeling helpless. "Oh, I don't know . . . I'm confused, out of a job . . ." Her voice trailed off.

He didn't speak for a long time, and she opened her eyes, needing to judge his reaction to what Brett had said about her broken engagement. She didn't want to admit that was the reason she'd come, but she couldn't kid herself about it any longer. She loved him and she wanted him to love her back. Now he knew she was free. What was he going to do about it?

He was watching her with eyes that were filled with an emotion she couldn't name. "I've already hired a manager, Anna."

She was standing there wrapped in his bedspread, practically begging for his love, and all he could say was, "I've already hired a manager"? Hurt and humiliated, she snapped, "Oh? Well, that's all I cared about—the job. And since you caught on to my sneaky trick to try and get back into your good graces, I'll be going. You're too clever for me!" She turned and struggled toward the door.

"Where do you think you're going in my bedspread?"

"I'm stealing it. What else would an Andrews want with anything of yours?" she retorted, too aware of his nearness for her peace of mind. "I fully expect you to press charges!"

Her feet came off the ground as he swept her into his arms. She reeled dizzily, grabbing his neck to keep from falling.

"I'd rather press kisses along that stubborn little jaw of yours," he whispered, his breath warm and inviting against her temple. "Are you sure Thad's out of your life?"

Disoriented, she was unable to form words and could only nod.

"That's damn good news," he murmured. "The night you left, I called him to tell him you were missing, and when you answered the phone sounding all sleepy and sweet..." He paused, his eyes sparking with the painful memory. Then he muttered roughly, "That was the worst damned pay back of my life."

She gasped, remembering that call. Remembering how she'd wished it had been Dusty on the line. "But...but Thad was only putting me up for the night! On his pull-out—"

"When I told you I loved you, Anna," he interrupted softly, "I meant for better or for worse. Forever."

She could hardly believe her ears. She rushed to explain, 'My mother made me promise, just before she died—'' she swallowed, working to finish ''—not to get involved with the wild type. She wanted me to find someone loyal and hard-working. Someone I could count on.''

"Your mother never met me, sugar." Then he kissed her, and the unexpected touch of his mouth made her quiver.

"Anna, Anna," he whispered against her mouth, "say you'll marry me."

She clung to him. "Oh, Dusty. I've loved you for so long." Nuzzling his chin, she said, "But I've run from fireworks men like you for so long. I'm frightened . . ."

"Don't be." He smiled. "What if I promise to be loyal and hardworking during the day and all fireworks at night?"

Her heart filled with joy, for she knew that he meant it, and she knew he was not anything like her father. Dusty Dare was a man she could count on for the rest of her days—and her nights. Lifting her lips to his, she conceded with a timid smile, "I think mother would be pleased."

The kiss they shared made Anna's heart soar. At last she could give herself over to the passion she'd held in check for so long.

In a delirious flash of happiness, she could see the future—her uncle Bud and Max playing checkers in the kitchen, eating warm slices of Max's rhubarb pie and spinning yarns about the good old days.

And she saw herself with her strong faithful fireworks man out in the round pen, teaching their children to train championship cutting horses—using his cattle and her oats! Giddy, she lifted her lips from his and teased, "Do I get to train Hazard now?"

He chuckled. "You and Frosty, for a while. When he retires in a few years and you're a world-class trainer yourself, you'll train Hazard, and Hazard's children and his grandchildren and his great-grandchildren.'' He kissed her lightly, his voice husky with desire. ''Unless you want our children to do that...''

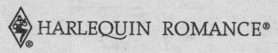

HARLEQUIN ROMANCE®

brings you

Stories that celebrate love, families and children!

Watch for our second Kids & Kisses title in *July*.

Island Child
by Roz Denny
Harlequin Romance #3320

Full of warmth, love and laughter. A story about what family *really means*, by the author of Romantic Notions *and* Stubborn as a Mule.

Sarah Michaels is a single mother with an eight-year-old son. She knows that a boy needs a male role model, a man to look up to and have fun with. That's why she signed up with Befriend an Island Child.

The agency sends Gabe Parker. Her son, Mike, is immediately crazy about him. But Sarah...well, Sarah's not so sure. The problem is, he reminds her of her ex-husband—in all the wrong ways.

Available wherever Harlequin books are sold.

Harlequin® Historical

LOOK TO THE PAST FOR
FUTURE FUN AND EXCITEMENT!

The past the Harlequin Historical way, that is. 1994 is going to be a banner year for us, so here's a preview of what to expect:

* The continuation of our bigger book program, with titles such as *Across Time* by Nina Beaumont, *Defy the Eagle* by Lynn Bartlett and *Unicorn Bride* by Claire Delacroix.

* A 1994 March Madness promotion featuring four titles by promising new authors Gayle Wilson, Cheryl St. John, Madris Dupree and Emily French.

* Brand-new in-line series: DESTINY'S WOMEN by Merline Lovelace and HIGHLANDER by Ruth Langan; and new chapters in old favorites, such as the SPARHAWK saga by Miranda Jarrett and the WARRIOR series by Margaret Moore.

* *Promised Brides,* an exciting brand-new anthology with stories by Mary Jo Putney, Kristin James and Julie Tetel.

* Our perennial favorite, the Christmas anthology, this year featuring Patricia Gardner Evans, Kathleen Eagle, Elaine Barbieri and Margaret Moore.

Watch for these programs and titles wherever Harlequin Historicals are sold.

HARLEQUIN HISTORICALS...
A TOUCH OF MAGIC!

Harlequin Books requests the pleasure of your company this June in Eternity, Massachusetts, for WEDDINGS, INC.

For generations, couples have been coming to Eternity, Massachusetts, to exchange wedding vows. Legend has it that those married in Eternity's chapel are destined for a lifetime of happiness. And the residents are more than willing to give the legend a hand.

Beginning in June, you can experience the legend of Eternity. Watch for one title per month, across all of the Harlequin series.

HARLEQUIN BOOKS...
NOT THE SAME OLD STORY!

This July,
Harlequin and Silhouette
are proud to bring you

WANTED: Husband
POSITION: Temporary
TERMS: Negotiable—but must be willing to live in.

And falling in love is definitely not part of the contract!

Relive the romance....

Three complete novels by your favorite authors—in one special collection!

TO BUY A GROOM by Rita Clay Estrada
MEETING PLACE by Bobby Hutchinson
THE ARRANGEMENT by Sally Bradford

Available wherever
Harlequin and Silhouette books are sold.

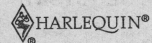 

Fifty red-blooded, white-hot, true-blue hunks
from every State in the Union!

Look for MEN MADE IN AMERICA! Written by some of
our most popular authors, these stories feature fifty of
the strongest, sexiest men, each from a different state in
the union!

Two titles available every other month at your favorite
retail outlet.

In May, look for:

KISS YESTERDAY GOODBYE by Leigh Michaels (Iowa)
A TIME TO KEEP by Curtiss Ann Matlock (Kansas)

In June, look for:

ONE PALE, FAWN GLOVE by Linda Shaw (Kentucky)
BAYOU MIDNIGHT by Emilie Richards (Louisiana)

You won't be able to resist MEN MADE IN AMERICA!

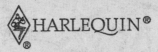

Where do you find hot Texas nights, smooth Texas charm and dangerously sexy cowboys?

Crystal Creek reverberates with the exciting rhythm of Texas.
Each story features the rugged individuals who live and love in the Lone Star state.

"...Crystal Creek wonderfully evokes the hot days and steamy nights of a small Texas community...impossible to put down until the last page is turned."
—*Romantic Times*

"...a series that should hook any romance reader. Outstanding"
—*Rendezvous*

"Altogether, it couldn't be better." —*Rendezvous*

Don't miss the next book in this exciting series.
SHAMELESS by SANDY STEEN

Available in July wherever Harlequin books are sold.

HARLEQUIN®

Don't miss these Harlequin favorites by some of our most distinguished authors!
And now, you can receive a discount by ordering two or more titles!

HT #25551	THE OTHER WOMAN by Candace Schuler	$2.99	☐
HT #25539	FOOLS RUSH IN by Vicki Lewis Thompson	$2.99	☐
HP #11550	THE GOLDEN GREEK by Sally Wentworth	$2.89	☐
HP #11603	PAST ALL REASON by Kay Thorpe	$2.99	☒
HR #03228	MEANT FOR EACH OTHER by Rebecca Winters	$2.89	☐
HR #03268	THE BAD PENNY by Susan Fox	$2.99	☐
HS #70532	TOUCH THE DAWN by Karen Young	$3.39	☐
HS #70540	FOR THE LOVE OF IVY by Barbara Kaye	$3.39	☐
HI #22177	MINDGAME by Laura Pender	$2.79	☐
HI #22214	TO DIE FOR by M.J. Rodgers	$2.89	☐
HAR #16421	HAPPY NEW YEAR, DARLING by Margaret St. George	$3.29	☐
HAR #16507	THE UNEXPECTED GROOM by Muriel Jensen	$3.50	☐
HH #28774	SPINDRIFT by Miranda Jarrett	$3.99	☐
HH #28782	SWEET SENSATIONS by Julie Tetel	$3.99	☐

Harlequin Promotional Titles

#83259	UNTAMED MAVERICK HEARTS (Short-story collection featuring Heather Graham Pozzessere, Patricia Potter, Joan Johnston)	$4.99	☐

(limited quantities available on certain titles)

DEDUCT:	AMOUNT	$
	10% DISCOUNT FOR 2+ BOOKS	$
	POSTAGE & HANDLING	$
	($1.00 for one book, 50¢ for each additional)	
	APPLICABLE TAXES*	$ _____
	TOTAL PAYABLE	$ _____
	(check or money order—please do not send cash)	

To order, complete this form and send it, along with a check or money order for the total above, payable to Harlequin Books, to: **In the U.S.:** 3010 Walden Avenue, P.O. Box 9047, Buffalo, NY 14269-9047; **In Canada:** P.O. Box 613, Fort Erie, Ontario, L2A 5X3.

Name: _____

Address: _____ City: _____

State/Prov.: _____ Zip/Postal Code: _____

*New York residents remit applicable sales taxes.
 Canadian residents remit applicable GST and provincial taxes.

HBACK-AJ